Culture on the Cuff
Declo Days and Other Tall Tales

Volume II

Front cover photo: Author's father and mother, two sisters Dora and May, and one of his two brothers, either Roy or Luke. St. Anthony, Idaho, 1913.

Culture on the Cuff
Declo Days and Other Tall Tales

Volume II

Dwight R. Droz

Scandia Patch Press
Poulsbo, Washington

Copyright © 2001 by Dwight R. Droz

All rights reserved. No part of this book may be reproduced or transmitted in any form or by any means, electronic or mechanical, including photocopying, recording, or by any information retreival system, without written permission of Scandia Patch Press.

Edited by:
    K. D. Kragen
    KaveDragen, Ink.
    kdkragen.com
    Bainbridge Island, Washington, USA

Product design/layout by K. D. Kragen
Cover design by Jerry George
Cover photo restoration by Jerry George
Image scanning/ photo editing and restoration
    by Lance P. Kragen and K. D. Kragen
Technical Advisor, Don Taylor

Unless otherwise noted, all sketches and illustrations are by the author, who studied art with Mr. Nelson at Southern Branch, University in Pocatello.

Scandia Patch Press
633 Northwest Scandia Road
Poulsbo, Washington 98370

Printed in the U.S.A.
10 9 8 7 6 5 4 3 2 1

Dedicated to the members of the Humbert-Droz family both the living and the deceased, especially May and Dora, my sisters.

"They go everywhere but they don't see nothin'."

CONTENTS

Introduction   2
Hymn of Harrison Valley   6
Buster Hound   48
One Nightingale, One Frog   50

1. Hard Times   56
2. The Cotterel Bride   64
3. The Spellcasters (Rain Follows the Plow)   92
4. Sons of the Land   102
5. Lost in a Storm   120
6. Snake Killer from Cheyenne   126
7. Taming the Wild   130
8. Baseballs and Hatchets   134
9. Rolling Up the Wire   138
10. The White Horse   142
11. Jenny and the Gypsy   144
12. Blind Barns   152
13. Flight From Cotterel   164
14. A Plat, A Town, A Dream   170

Bibliography   176

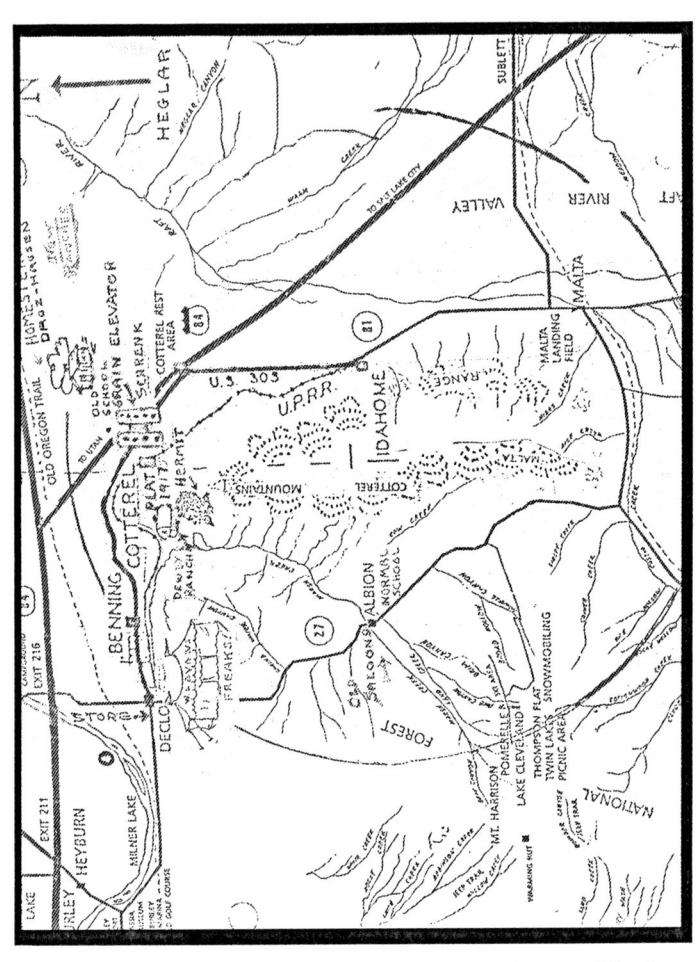

Southern Idaho, including Cotterel, Heglar, Albion, and Declo.
Note Droz homestead, at top of map, right on the Old Oregon Trail.

Cotteral, Heglar and Albion

Introduction

There is a town in Idaho named Albion. It was once the county seat of a vast strip of desert and meadow land before Burley, Rupert or Twin Falls emerged. The town of Declo, seven or so miles below, marks the spot where my family settled in after WW I. It was there I learned to drive a four-string, tugging groaning wagon out of autumn fields.

At a time when the world was aflame with *The Great War*, and even the pages of the *Burley Bulletin* were filled with stories such as "Peace Efforts of Wilson Abandoned" and "Austrian Archduke and Wife Slain," in those days Albion was the gifted place that brought us culture and hope. Verlene Powell, Curator of Albion Historical Museum, sent me old clippings and data of the early days. Here is a good example:

This picture features an early stage-run, but it was the Kelton trail, linking Utah and Boise, right through Albion, which was the most direct route ever designed to move freight. It had twenty stations and ran for 232 miles. A real mover! Albion was the Home Station for the "Kelton Trail."

The Kelton Road was a historic run, nearly

obliterated, now. How they carved such a short and straight trail baffles me yet. This moment in time was Albion's finest hour!

I remember seeing one *most unusual* person named Willie Sears. I knew both his daughters. At that point of time, I did not realize how fast the clock of history ticks. Yes, he rode in the Pony Express! I was completely unaware of it, so I never asked him a single, useful question!

What else did Willie do, you might ask? He was the "relayer" who rode a lathered horse over Albion's last ridge with a historic pardon for Diamondfield Jack. No, I'm not cooking this up!

Southwest of what is now Burley, just west of the headwaters of Rock Creek lies historic "Deadline Ridge." A gentleman's agreement of 1890 posited sheep herders would stay east of the ridge, and cattle ranchers would graze west of the ridge. Jackson Lee Davis, who picked up the name "Diamondfield" in a boggled mining venture, was hired by Sparks & Harrell Cattle Company in 1895 to patrol the ridge.

Jack, a garrulous spider soon was ensnared in a web involving two sheepherders who had strayed over the line. From that incident a range war developed and he was a central figure in this event. Though short in stature, Jack cast a long shadow over years of Idaho history and established friends, even among his jailers. Albion still remembers him. David H. Grover's has written the authoritative biography, *Diamondfield Jack: A Study in Frontier Justice* (The Lancehead Series, Nevada & the West, 1968). As we so often say, history surpasses fiction. This is a marvelous tale, and Albion is its focal point.

Now, for the rest of the story 'bout "a jewel of a

school." The students of that sainted campus gazed on slopes where ranches sunned; the view of Harrison's peaks gave it the grandeur you learned to savor. When you take Nature hikes or skimmed the slopes (they had a ski class) you eventually followed a well-defined trail through open glades and quaking aspen dells to drink the clear waters of Lake Cleveland nestling under Harrison's snowy peaks. No campus I've trod had a grander view or more devoted teachers. That was my opinion the year I attended, an analysis shared by many of my Declo classmates who trained there and went on to lifetime teaching careers.

> Above it lies the slopes and fells
> Of Howell's Creek where Beauty dwells!
> In high July the Sphinx moth sups
> In lanes of blue-flamed lupine-cups!

One of the first school buildings in Albion.

The pride of Albion, District No. 3 School, built in the late 1880s – at the end of East Market Street.

Maps of the Kelton Road vary a little, but the significant point is this. That road was a direct route for freight and mail, a marvel of the time. There were stations about every 12 miles where fresh teams replaced the weary ones as passengers embarked or "de-staged." The actual distance was only 232 miles from the rail depot at Kelton, Utah to the Boise, Idaho terminal. This distance is hard to realize when you consider the rough terrain involved. You can truly say, Albion had foresight and spirit beyond belief![1]

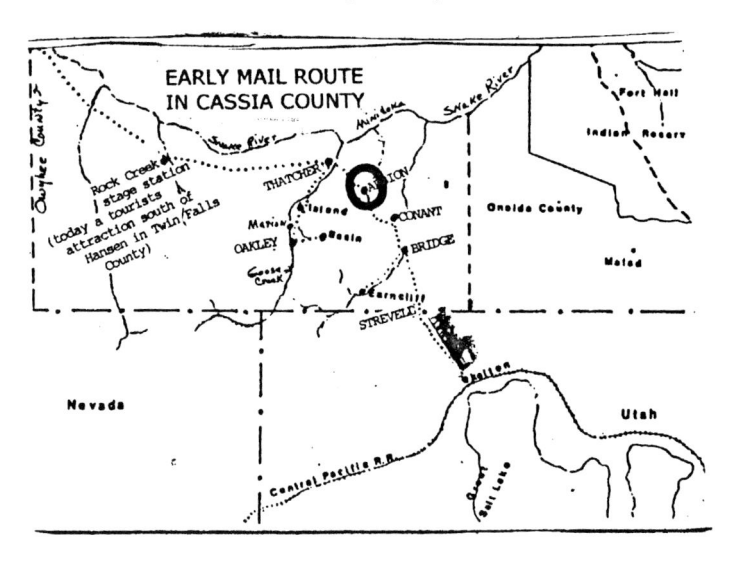

The Kelton Road. Albion is circled in the upper middle.

---

[1] This data was cheerfully provided by Verlene L. Powell, Curator of Albion's Historical Museum. Thank you Albion! Once, I shared the sound, enjoyed the sights, of your fine "citadel" on the heights.

HYMN OF HARRISON VALLEY

Prologue

The cold moon gleams on Cassia's hill:
The somber crags are hushed and still,
And steeples of the sleeping town[1]
Are silvered spikes by star beams strewn.

---

[1] Refers to Albion town in 1930's. A charming place with Albion Normal School providing a grand view of Mt. Harrison's peaks.

I
Remember The Valley

Here by the hearth where the andirons gleam
And the smoke blues out like wisps of steam
Where an old great-clock, so solemn, ticks
To sharp reports of the apple sticks—
Burning blue and gold in the ruddy heat—
I love to feel a reverent beat
Of old, dear things that seem so far
As lamplight blends with a distant star.
...
This dog, asleep on the mat of my door,
Reminds of a sire, of a sire of yore;
And swallows rustling within the eaves
Bring back lost days and falling leaves.
...
Where the long lane leads to a broad canal
The larks rehearse their madrigal;
On orchard boughs the robins trill
When morning wakes the dew drenched hill.
The sleeping rose awakes to nod
Across the way to goldenrod,
And lupines toss their palmy leaves
Where fencerows guard the gathered sheaves.

An 88 year memory of Albion Church. Tiny flowrets, natives called "Bread and Butter," carpet the sage in this sandy lot. No other soul was about that day. I gazed on magic Mt. Harrison. My replica of them is bland, I fear. The church may have not had a steeple, but I put one there in case my memory is weakened by time. I think there were wild pinks in those rings too. I do know there were purple horse heads in marshy meadows nearby.

II

Harrison Vale

On distant hills of Harrison
That Autumn's grasses billow on,
The lazy, low October mists
Lie, dozing o'er her granite schists,
Or priestly Spring barefoots the snow
Where fragile, wide-eyed daisies blow;
While far below, on bosomed plains,
The buds are swelled with April rains.
...
On a peak's far heights, the eagles mark,
Where snow drifts chain the granite scarp
That flaming sunsets pour upon,
Now flames the glory of the dawn;

The bright stars glow like twinkling shields
And cast their lances on the fields.
...
The vales below they dot with light
Upon the still midsummer's night
Or probe the depths of Cleveland's pond
Like shimmering silks of Trebisond;[1]
As o'er it all, the quiet hill
Re-echoes to the splashing rill
Where forests weave a jeweled chain
(That o'er the timbered slope is lain)
Where aspens cloud the rocky lair
And fill the glen with murmurs there.

This lovely butterfly files along the trail to Lake Cleveland.
15. *Parnassius clodius altaurus, male.* Dollarside Summit, Sawtooth Mts., ID, July 23, 1954. **16.** *Parnassius clodius altaurus, female.* Trail Creek, Sawtooth Mts., ID, July 21, 1954.

III

<u>The Garden and Corral</u>

The marmalade and pickled quince,
And tiers of apple, evidence
Of rich fruition from our field,
Lay in the cellar's fortress sealed.
The golden stores of pumpkins, bright,
(From which we carved a leering sight)

---

[1] A fanciful domain, perhaps in Hindustan.
[2] From: *The Butterflies of North America*, Plate 68, William H. Howe, editor (New York, 1975).

And rows of bottled plum and pear—
And peach and raspberry were there:
The hams that father cured in brine
And apple ciders rich and fine—
And all the goods our cellar filled
Were from the Cassia's earth we tilled.

...

From rustic lengths of garden wall
I hear the purling creek o'erfall
As blackbirds burst their carillon
Down where the rushbound hedges run.
The lark repeats it on the lea—
Repeats in classic minstrelsey,
And katydids along the hedge
Hum softly at the garden edge.

...

---

[1] I raised pumpkins all my life. Little tots loved to pick them a generation ago. They still do. Larry Steagall, a Bremerton Sun photographer, snapped the left harvester on October 27, 1987. Steve Zugswert, another staffer, shot the miss on the right, October 27, 1964, and labeled his work "Mahem of the Pumpkin Patch!" We thank the Bremerton SUN for permission to use their photos.

The bat weaves through, at twilight's fall,
The patchwork of that leafy hall,
Through pear and poplar's dappling shade
As velvet shadows cross the glade,
As night slips down from shaded peaks,
And ebbs the sun's last, paling streaks.
...
The weary bull then lays him down
And bovine like, awaits the crown
Of morning fire from the sun,
And cares not that his day is done.
The kine that from the meadows plod
Are laden with the fruits of sod,
And from the straw shed lowing, now,
Summon the lad upon the mow.
...
The weary teams hunch as they drink;
Their muzzles brush a rippling brink
As lightly as some feather down;
Then, heads upthrown, they wheel around
With one last burst of effort willed
To reach the mangers, brimming-filled,
To nuzzle at the plumpest grains,
Forgetting tyranny of reins.

IV
The Fields

How often my brown dog and I
Have waded fields of clover, nigh,
Or watched their stricken phalanx fall
That round the hissing blade would sprawl
To rout the fieldmouse from his lair,
The weasel with malignant glare,
The pheasant with her half grown brood,
Protesting from their solitude:
And on the fields the plow had crushed
We nurtured life from barren dust
Till waving legions masked the clod
In destiny ordained of God.
...
How bright the sheaves; how blue the sky!
Afar, where distant summits lie,
I hear again the insect wings
Of distant summer carolings:
The lowing herd—in pastures near,
An echo of the rill is clear;
The blessed note of plainting dove,
The zephyr, whispering in the grove,
The sparrows, murmuring in content,
'Mid sounds where rustling corn is bent,
All blended in a peaceful scene
On rolling oceans of green.

...
The burdock on the flowering bank
Met nettles at the willows flank
The great bull thistle, rearing high,
That weaving caterpillars tie,
With wild sweetclover stalks would sun
Where yellow banks of sunflower run.
All these that solitude inspires
Were filled with chants of feathered choirs.
...
The chant of frogs beyond the leven[1]
Seemed to fill the starry heaven,
And floating grace of monarch red
At noon poised o'er the milkweed bed;
While *rutulus*, that swallowtail,[2]
Went skimming o'er the lilac-vale
Till, fairy like, their being seems
To glorify those childhood dreams.

---

[1] A lawn.
[2] *Papilio rutulus*. From: William Howe, *The Butterflies of North America*, New York, 1975.

VI
The Poplars

I'll ne'er forget the poplars, tall,
Where moonlight etched their twinkling wall—
When violet shadows they interned
And stars upon their summits burned—
Who marched up from the garden's edge
To gesture by my window ledge;
And, rooted deep within me still,
Are lessons of their pliant will—
The tenderness with which they gave
Their leaves unto an earthly grave:
Their pious voices prayed aloud,
They, fearless, faced the bursting cloud,
They chastely fought the sensuous wind
And taught me grace is Nature's end.
...
Their supple boughs reached out to me
(What lad but would not climb a tree!)
As there the oriole I spied
Amid the branches, spreading wide.
I gazed on roofs and streams below,
Observed my knowledge with them grow;
Saw branches die and scars o'erheal,
And watched the planets o'er them wheel:
Watched machinations of Polaris,
The axis of a mighty Ferris;
Or marked, where over topped their stair,
The gleaming Cassiopeia's Chair;
Saw spring's adorn or frosts denude—
And cried beneath their branches, rude.
...
Though years have passed, I thrill to see
And dearly love a poplar tree
That builds a fortress from the sun

And strives to shield where arbors run.
It bows to clouds its leafy spires,
And vibrates to the feathered choirs.
It does not droop like the lazy willow,
But is a proud, stout-hearted fellow
Who loves to spread a chest-of-leaves
Protectively 'round cottage eaves.
There is no dwelling—be it mean—
That does not share that noble green
Without reflecting in its glow
Upon the plains of Idaho.

Perhaps no fancier would praise it.
But water touching earth will raise it;
Children will not pass it lightly;
And sparrows quarrel in it nightly.
Cats with grasping claws climb up
And robins teeter on the top.
It does not claim the birch's beauty
But shows a reverence to duty
That does not shirk at menial labors—
Like holding fences up twixt neighbors.
This tree's a friend to fowls and frogs,
And don't you even mention dogs.
If plants could love the wind and sun,
A poplar tree would be the one!

VII
Farm Life

In full view of the mountain's face
Our father built our dwelling place.
He railed off sage to clear the land
And saw new waters touch the sand
From out the lateral ditches pried,
Hauled timber from the mountain side
To build those straw sheds warm and stout;
And soon young calves and colts o'er-ran
Our palisaded pasture glen.
The crow went winging o'er the corn
And drifting hawks surveyed our barn;
Rodents in the grain did creep
And coyotes forayed on the sheep.
...
On weaving plows we coursed the land
When four-abreast horses strained their band
On frosty morns—through sleeting day;
For naught deterred our destiny—
No one knows how we labored here
Who has not meshed a cranky share
Into the earth. He does not know
Who has not plowed in driving snow
How long the hours, how drab the day,
Or how much for the sun we pray
Who till the fields on raw springtide
When ice still chokes the countryside.

The horses—they are noble things
Whose willing spirits face the stings
Of flurried hail and chilling sleet:
I watched their rhythmic, striving feet,
To bade them rest whene'er I could
    While speculating solitude.
On warmth of home fires I wistfully thought,
    And pondered on our toilsome lot—
Of why the rich worked less than we!
Then larks rang out with minstrelsey
    In spite of rain and driving snow:
I heard the young lambs bleating low,
To feel the surge of spring was near;
No matter now that skies were drear.

VIII

Father And The Farm

A rambling farmhouse looked upon
    The snowy peaks of Harrison
Where papa built it, firm and sound,
    With poplar saplings all around
And willow twigs with care implanted
That make our country lanes enchanted.
    Shaggy barked, green juniper
    He hauled from off the rocky spur

Of Cotterel knolls—and still they stand
To guard the fencerows of our land,
A steeple for the caroling lark.
There, owls lament long after dark—
Young, robins lilt their songs anew
While sparrows gossip, summers through.
...
That farmer loved a saw and square;
He'd frame a shelter anywhere.
His father taught
My dad just how a craftsman ought
To level sills, cut rafters true—
And papa was a millwright too.
In Switzerland he learned the way
They build a big lodge—or chalet.
He told us tales of stalwart men
Who rappelled down some Alpine glen.

A. Sixteenth-century rapier
B. Italian bronze-hilted sword

How brave and bold
Were those adventurers of old,
Like one old soldier's[1] body found

---

[1] Vieillard is a Swiss name for and old man. This old soldier was warned at the inn not to cross the pass but tarry a while. He said

18

With a ring of wolf bones circled 'round!
Beside his skull lay a broken sword;
We listened close to every word.
He knew how children loved a tale
And by the hour he'd regale
With episodes that proved, in truth,
The doubtless mischief of his youth.
...
At night, when outer gales would beat.
We loved to gather 'round his feet
To listen to a golden store
Of old Swiss history and lore:
Of how our grandsire hung a bell[1]
Upon a church in Neuchâtel—
On a narrow scaffold, lone, he stood
Grandfather hung it; no other could.
He'd watch our eyes grow big the while
And how his twinkling eyes would smile.
...
He joined Alaska's search for gold
And talked of death and fearsome cold
Where awesome Borealis ran
Above the skies of Ketchikan.
Though grown infirm, his eyes would gleam
When he beheld a mountain stream.
His shortcomings we understood
Forgiven by o'erbalanced good.

---

timber wolves did not matter and headed for the pass in a driving snow.

[1] Story was my great granfather was strongest man in the village. He was injured in a fall from a scaffold on a chalet. He was pierced through the abdomen by a huge sliver of wood. After long hospitalization, he was swinging down street and saw two men striving to hang a bell on a narrow scaffold. Great grandfather called, "Come down; I'll hang the bell." He did. Both my parents mentioned that incident many times.

An angry wit to lies he bared;
He was with honesty interred.
Earth's simple, loving earnest one,
He labored well; the work is done.

IX
The Family

My mother who is aging now[1]
Did unto us her life endow
With quiet courtesy and grace;
She sought to make our home a place
Of cultural things. She was imbued
With poetry and zeal for good:
Mother tended garden—loved the sod,
Attributed all things to God,
Doctored the sick and strove to be
The tutor of morality.
More than a common farmer's wife,
She brought significance to life.

...

---

[1] Olga Humbert-Droz died in Santa Monica, California at age of 107 and 1/2 years.

We learned to watch the clouds unveil
And heard the ranting of the gale
With sharing joys in fond abode
Where books upon the shelves were stowed
Like food upon our cellar shelves—
And so we entertained ourselves.
How many quaint old volumes, rare,
Were stored in her collection there:
From Poe to Wordsworth, Keats and Dickens;
And all the lore that fancy quickens
When sleet upon the casement spatters,
While fairy tales of ghouls and satyrs,
In far off lands—by time enmisted
Our necromantic dreams enlisted.

These visions, fair, I owe to her
And to the sister who would spur
My childish fancy when she read
To me while oft I lay abed,
Or to us all, assembled there.
The lamplight gleamed upon her hair,
Her voice was soft and redolent
And with a soft inflection lent
That caught the texture of a theme

To make it credible to dream.
We were implored to come to bed
(Another chapter, then she read.)
We sadly watched the book laid by
And summoned slumber with a sigh.

X

Playmates

Remembrances of Childhood Days—
I see again the sunlit ways
On paths that wound where cattle fed—
And mysteries of an old straw shed.
The fields were wide as palace halls.
Turquoise skies o'ercapped the walls
Of ripening corn. How full the joys
Of freckled, sunburned barefoot boys
And girls who were as fond as we
Of wandering lanes of pastures free.
The lark sang with us merrily.
(The creek laughed loudly on the lee.)
And suns with wreath'ed cheer looked down
On denims blue. or a gingham gown.

I see again my sweet Pauline
With innocence of mild thirteen,
Fair Edith with the clear brown eyes,

And Louise, often moved to sighs
If any heartless word was said:
O, happy children, where have led—
(Those paths that parted us in turn)?
What did you lose? What did you earn?
Poor Willie to the grave was sent
Before he'd even earned the rent..
Thomas in the war was thrown,
And Elsa lies 'neath a cumb'ring stone,
While Pat and Dale[1] who were like kin
Within the sod are molded in.
...
And fair Elisse, her parents gone
By cancer stricken, wandered on—
I know not where. The mothering touch,
The childhood faded—there is much
Of life we dare not dwell upon;
Shed a tear if you must and then be gone.
Men must not cry! Fools may recite
A prattler's truths. There is no light
Can penetrate the depths of Time.
Death bars the door and ends the rhyme.

XI

---

[1] Pat Grewell and Dale MeCartney, two high school classmates who died before graduation.

Reincarnation

Go back to the hearth where andirons gleam.
Beside an open fire I dream
To fancy I see a radiant face
Of Glenice with that youthful grace
Who smiled on all with girlish wiles
That brought a chorus of our smiles.
How sweet she was! Her youthful mien
Held pride and carriage of a queen
Whose wisdom seemed beyond her years.
(She knew how smiles could master tears
Before her years half reached a score
While I scarce learned in twenty more.)
So some are blessed with laughter, wise,
To cure a world of ills and sighs,
When some seem cursed to walk alone
By pity, fear or pride undone.

Yet time is brief that men must mourn,
Thank God that joy is yet reborn
And pattering children's feet will trod
Above them slumbering in the sod;
More Willies, bold, and Alices, fair,
Play hopscotch in the village square;
And timorous Joans and tremulous Jeannes

Roam, breathlessly our county greens.
See Joes and Marys look askance,
Watching a redskin horde advance
With muskets poised and sabers drawn;
Now, comes the battle of Meuse—Argonne[1]
While toiling fathers pause and smile
And feel the tug of youth beguile.
...
Their light. must never fade from earth.
The re-enactment of their mirth
Echoes from year to year—and Death
Grapples but conquers not all breath:
It shakes the stem of flower and fruit;
It gnaws at life in every shoot;
Yet green waves cloud the hill and glen:
And mankind, scourged, can rise again
To dream and sing to voiceless stars,
To fusillade th' infinite bars
Of Time and Space with questionings:
Beyond all corporeal things,
As from the past our future draws
To frame a world of rules and laws.

XII

Deserts

The purple, brooding deserts lay
To edge upon our fields of hay.
Their shadowed slopes and rocky swales
We roamed in heat and beating gales—

---

[1] A battle of World War I was not fought with muzzle loaders and swords, but you make do with even less when you're a child of nine or so.

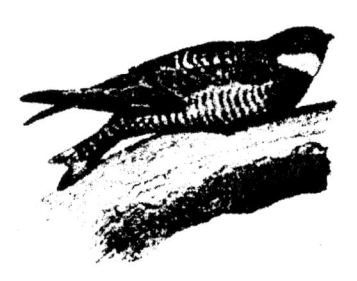

Nighthawk, *Chordeiles minor*

Heard nighthawks booming there at dusk
And breathed in deep the honeyed musk,
The spic'ed scents, on fragrant winds,
Or, fearless, roamed a trail that binds
The vast unknown. 'Neath star spun skies
We saw a glo'bed moon uprise
Where shadowed cedars bent[1] with age,
Prayed solemnly above the sage
A litany of wind, and rain,
And hope that storms will come again.

Our dogs—they loved a desert chase,
When long-limbed rabbits they would race
While through the spiced sage we ran
To circumvent their caravan.

---

[1] Technically, a scrub juniper that is closely allied to cedar. Many people call them cedar.

Beyond the slope our eyes would mark
A whip of dust—a frenzied bark
Would drift down to us from the ridge
As, horses clattering o'er the bridge,
We strove to follow their advance
As, now and then, we caught a glance;
Would hear their far off, swelling throats
Echo despair—then triumph notes—
A final cry—a sudden hush—
Soft voiced, cries the hermit thrush.
...
A crushed, limp form—the rabbit's blood—
The wound that gaped from whence the flood
Of life had ebbed—all these we knew,
Observed our hounds like vampires drew
The heart warm meats in scissored teeth
To crush the vitals underneath.
...
We knew, we saw (though children then)
How early tragedy began,
How lust and fury, intertwined,
Entrench themselves within the mind.
...
The seething snake with venom'd dart
Implanted venom in our heart;
The cruel-eyed weasel drew our hate
And traps we planted in his wait.

Weasel, *Mustela frenata*

And who will change what was to be
Perhaps the plan of Deity,
Perhaps the curse of him who fell!
Whoever, he has taught us well
Who taught us love of guns and swords,
And subtle, sweet, deceitful words,
The rancors hidden by a smile,
And claws of lust we glove in guile;
The piety that glows without
To hide the penuries of doubt,
The shackled pride that restless springs
In caged ambition to be kings—
To clutch the golden tress of Time
And make the Gods of hate sublime.
...
And who shall change the fated plan
That makes the tyrant of the man—
The icy mail, the harpy sword,
The lance that to the breast is gored?
What glory? Nay, what carnage thine,
Vile product of the concubine
By devils wooed! Thou mate of whore
Who wears the gilded braid of WAR!
...
With faltering faith; in tears enslaved—
May immortality be engraved
On hearts of men—set spirits free;
Might Heaven grant this gift to me.

XIII

By Banks Of The Snake

On the broad Snake's wide redresses
where the cool springs well in creases
Where the green perch leaps from cover
In the haunts of quail and plover,

There the bare-kneed, sunburned yokel
Whistles while the river, vocal,
Chants a melody that tipples
Whorls of Mayflies on the ripples.

In the dew-starched airs of dawning,
Where the lithe-limbed frogs are spawning,
There[1] as romping lads we tarried,
Searched where arrowheads lay buried,
Saw where crows to nests commuted,
Sacked and stoned, and pried and looted!
Here the starlight skips through rushes
In among the current brushes
As the swallows murmur over
Fresh from bursting fields of clover.
...
Have you seen the willows flailing
To a thunderhead's regaling
Where the marshes toss their mains up
(Like wild mares from where the plains drop)
As the wild bees sip in bevies
Down among the grassy levees?
...
Here the sundial, dandelion,

---

[1] A special place by Petersen's Island, perhaps two miles east of Declo. We called it The Drop—and no other spot has an equal charm in my mind. It was above the bank of Snake River and a pirate retreat of renown for small boys bent on fun and mayhem.

Lifts, a hoary headed scion,
'Mongst flagellant, buttery fellows
Decked in bright arrays-of-yellows.
Here the skipper[1] flits unduly
Through the haunted, whispering tulle
And the monarch, drifting under,
Eyes his marshy realm-of-wonder.

Have you seen the gilt moon, steeping,
Bridge the brook with crescents, leaping,
As the bawdy streamlet chuckles
Through the rough, termagant ripples
While the thickets hush to listen
Where the sparkling moonbeams glisten?
...
When the heart of earth is beating

---

[1] Skipper, a family of the butterflies that is characterized by a fat, stubby body with comparatively small wings.

To the softly-murmured greeting
Of the night gusts in the willow,
Hear the night owl's wavering query
Calling somber-voiced and eerie,
On the ridge beyond the corn
Where, now, a pale rayed star is born.

Skippers have chubby bodies and short wings.

Have you heard the whispering cadence
Of the willow's lithe evadence
As it weaves through wending rushes
From the reach of gray sagebrushes
Where the sego lily, pompous,
Is a far, star-pointing compass,
While the thickets hush to listen
When the yellow moon has risen?
Here the lark his trembling breast breaks
To cajole the falling snowflakes
Until lilacs bud and follow
Spring's green verdured hill and hollow
Where the green snake bathes him daily
And the song thrush warbles gaily.

XIV

Meadowlark

O, how fair these wildernesses
Where the clear spring breaks in cresses
When the broad Snake, shoreward wheeling,
Laves upon the willow, kneeling,
As the blackbird, child of ebon,
Bursts the solitudes of heaven.
Here the lazy bullfrog dozes

As the lowing Hereford poses.
O, how swift the dragonflies flair
Where their multifidous eyes were
Filled with bulbous, flashing jets in—
That had mystic, myriad sets in!
Flames of blue, they nestled over
Ponded golden rod and clover
While vee-throated larks went singing,
Down the flowered fencerows winging.

Anthem of my soul! Spring goddess!
Sweet, wild lark, with songs applaud us
As the vaulted wide blue o'er us
Brims the heart with thy sweet chorus!
Burst thy trembling breast, thou angel
Who are pastureland's evangel—
Crush us in melodious raptures
As thy art, unwritten captures
What the fluted wind entreats you—
"Sing again," the groves beseech you
Where the dull-eyed snake is sleeping
By the brook's white crescent's leaping,
As the marshes toss their mains
(Like wild mares from off the plains)
When the pink rose floods the hollow
And the tinkling sheep bells follow.

XV
The Sorrel And Her Colt

How often with my sorrel mare
I rode from off the desert bare
To where those rim-rock spires thrust,
Surmounted by the acrid dust,
So bright, the beaming sun peered down,
And wild sunflowers smiled around.
Up we climbed the rim-rock steep
To where the valley lay asleep,
And distant water shimmered far
Blue-glowing like a vitriol star:
There, junipers, like gnomes of Pan,
Stood, dwarfish figures of a man.

They marked the outposts of a wood
In realms of whispering solitude.
An echoing ax rang through the glen,
That ever-present sound of men
Who cannot stand to see a wood
But they must break its hold for good,
Stamp out the sego lily, rare,
To make our deserts doubly bare
All for a bit of kindling stick,
Or spindly posts to fence a "crick,"
To check a mule or blundering hog.
They go in raptures for a log—

Those little men by shovels bent
Whose lives like bumbling moles are spent
Who could not leave a tree for grace
As if they desecrate a place!
...
Full forty miles they hauled their wood
And tore the forests out for good
That were not plentiful to start
For stable pole, and beam, and cart;
Or when a struggling shrub was spied,
Though it was scrubbed and nearly died,
They'd spend a morn to cut it free—
And get more chips and stump than tree—
Then drag the poor dismembered joke
Back home to please the womenfolk
To make a fire to boil the meat
And give their poor, blind souls some heat:
And spindly aspen shook, of course,
From axes sawing at their source;
When posts, within the ground they stood
For three years, maybe, doing good,
And rotted out full well in four—
And aspined hillsides were no more!

How well that sorrel mare could run
As on horseback in the burning sun
We cut across the talused slope
In high abandon, on full lope,
Though yawning chasms groaned beneath:
(How Fate must surely gnash her teeth
To think of all the risks we took)
But old Maud knew it like a book,
Could dodge the boulders, miss the stump,
And slide down talus "a-la-rump"
With wisdom range bred broomtails find
Whose instincts far surpass the mind;
And with a nonchalance encored
Her agile feats as though quite bored.
Though quail or sagehen made her start,
Her feet were skilled, subconscious art.

I trusted her, that equine elf,
More surely than I'd trust myself—
In storm or icy underfoot,
In broiling stream or frosted rut,
On upthrust stone—she knew them all,
Cared not a whit if she should fall,
And loved to run at skelter pace,
Or cut a gatepost like a base;
But wire made her quite insane
As though it were the spawn of Cain—
And if I swore, it was because
I couldn't lead her where it was.

Though it were down and bound with grass,
A full ten feet around she'd pass;
And though I'd arch myself and pull,
She was as stubborn as a bull;
Till, if at last she bolted over,
It was as though a demon drove her.

...

Her colt was stringhalt;[1] that may be
One reason for her chicanery
And terror of the barb'ed steel,
For who knows what a mare can feel?
The colt was maimed until he died—
A fine young colt he was, and wide
And sound in chest and good in heart.
(How oft' perfection fails in part.)
His hind leg joint was cut to bone,
And three good legs were spoiled by one!
And yet he tried to work, poor brute—
He was the one we had to shoot,
And it was not a pleasant thing
To hear that deathly bullet sing
Or see him struggle to the sod—
I think a horse was made by God
To share with man—and that is why
I cried to see that sorrel die.

XVI

School

I see, as though but yesterday
The red brick school across the way
Where intersecting roads combined

---

[1] The middle joint of his right hind leg was locked tight. He would raise the leg and drop it like an automaton.

To stamp its fortress in my mind.
With bitter hatred of its bell
(I dreaded that conjuring knell).
The lagging hours marked my fate
When, prone to dream, I dallied, late.
...
How many hours upon its stair
I entered with foreboding where
A stern faced master, waiting, stood
With well worn rule of stout hardwood
In my await. I learned to see
School's much-praised joys were not for me
When through the blank faced panes I spied
Free larks upon the pastures, wide;
Or fretted through the early spring
To watch the white lambs gamboling.

Declo School

My schoolmates were a motley crowd,
All denim clad except a proud,
Small few who by some quirk of fate
A cultured home did emulate
Who always got the highest mark.
They never had to stay near dark
Because a spitwed went askew.
They never were the ones who threw
Erasers or a bit of chalk,
And *wouldn't think* to cheat or balk.

...
My sums were seldom apropos
To what the answer book could show;
Lynn Massachusetts—boots and shoes[1]
Was no geography I could use;
War of 1812, 1492,
Were all the history dates I knew;
Though I read and spelled among the best,
I was impervious to the rest.
...
I injured one hip when l was small
So l wasn't desirable at all
For manly sports and hectic fun.
I'd scramble along but couldn't run
So recess time was rather grim.
"He's a bummer, boys! Don't mess with him!"
Well, never mind, my thoughts rotated
On fantasies, nature created,
Traversing lanes of larks and brooks,
Devouring non-pedantic books.
And, now and then, I garnered friends—
Like me—made out of odds and ends.
Girls really were our nemesis,
But didn't matter much, I guess.

VII

The Bully

How well the bully I recall
Who fought so well with one and all
And drove all bargains with his fist.
He loved to give your arm a twist
To lord it over all the school—

---

[1] Geographies often listed products of a city or region. What does Lynn make now?

And always played the biggest fool.
He knew all kinds of devil's tricks
Incorporating stones and sticks!
There was nothing too vulgar, or too lewd,
His repertory to include.

That rawkus laughter, uncontrolled,
The marrow of his mirth extolled
Exposing, bare, a vacuous mind
To conscience mute, and deaf—and blind.
Still, at times, in spite of him,
He did the milk of kindness skim,
All unforeseen, because, in part,
His evil genius failed the art.
...
Upon some gala Sunday morn
He'd single "sissies" out to scorn
Enroute to church—a dressed up dandy,
Take his collection[1], plus any candy
To share with followers that ran
Behind his heels—that favored clan!
Upon the eve of Halloween
His mass destruction could be seen:
He poached in any private yard

---

[1] Coins of course.

To push the privy over hard,
Leaving the whole in ghastly rout,
Prying gatepost hinges out,
Scattering pickets, a fowl or shoat
(Causing neighbors to grab a neighbor's throat [1])
Or tied some cow where a mule was "lifted";
In deviltry the lad was gifted!
...
He bragged of chewing or drinking liquor,
Said it never made him sick, n'er
Ever fazed-his-constitution!
He swore in every tongue but "Rooshian,"
Liked to fancy he was rougher
Than any hoodlum 'round—and tougher;
Rode a horse like he was mad
And would have liked to tromp his dad,
For in this art he never rested,
Perhaps in fear of being bested
By some newcomer he admitted
Into the clan who counterfeited
Some patent sin the maestro taught him;
Then the bragging chump forgot him.
...
The force that drove him has me puzzled
As, run amuck, he lied and guzzled,
Smoked, told lewd tales indiscreetly
And played a hellion completely.
Did careworn stepdame and drinking father
Fester the wound of losing his mother?[2]
Did inward stress befoul and plague
That soul—although the reason's vague?
He's dead, poor lad; don't judge too tritely—

---

[1] Quarrelsome neighbors blame such antics on the man next door.
[2] His mother died in the flu epidemic following World War I. A common occurrence. He missed her love.

Or demean his character impolitely—
Lest kinder facets, undisplayed
In those routines, leave you dismayed.
...
In spite of wrongs, let judgment brief
Ascribe some worth this pranksome thief.
He certainly would have been less of a dolt
With a dribble of care you'd offer a colt.
Or a tool of good brand. We oil wrenches with care;
Then yank-children around-by-the nape as it were!
The world is chock full of misguided intention;
Someone failed the boy—whatever you mention.

XVIII

Instructors

Most principals were learned men
Whose erudition served "pro tem"
In jurisprudent starched cravat
And pompous air of this and that.
(The little import of their place
Was quite apparent in each face.)
As through the much-thumbed text they plied
To read verbatim if defied.
The text was gospel through and through
Whose maxims were "quite-trite-but-true;"

For books were law! The text, in state,
Like a corpse, we very, literally ate
The sickness that I oft would find
Was indigestion of my mind;
But, by and large, the class was good;
My schoolmates said they understood.

Those teachers were of every kind
That e'er oppressed the human mind:
More wise of brain than warm of heart,
More fond of money than of art,
Seeking effect of form and grace,
Criteria of a country place—
More puffed with pomp than graced with truth;
Thinking their age impressed our youth,
Oft much unread and much unwise[1]
They brought their world before our eyes.
Quite soon we learned to fear their wrath
(What rancid words stern justice hath.)
Who taught us with stern glance, or blows[2]
Or with condolence, if they chose,
As by imploring, threats and force
The colt is taught to be a horse.

---

[1] This passage criticizes some teachers; by no means all of them.
[2] One teacher (name withheld) loved to hit us with a hardwood ruler or a wooden pointer, good, sound whacks.

Once I knew a dead eye at Mr. Hebold's place; he won all my marbles with a rather wooden face. Next, he moved to Rupert, earning plenty tubs of dough. Friend, if you are prone to wobble, count on twenty years of snow!

...

Yet, some there were, a blessed few,
Whose tact and kindness did outdo
Their brothers of the beetling brow;
And I am thankful even now
To think of those who understood
That boys, at best, are none too good,
Who viewed with tolerance our faults,
Our tops, and toys, and spitwad vaults[1],
Our gums and candies, tucked in cheek
That made it difficult to speak
Without discovery when we tried
To whisper secrets on the side
To help a neighbor solve his sums;
Or, palming marbles twixt our thumbs,
We bragged of how some "taw" would shoot
So we could swap a substitute.

...

When schools can teach a love that girds
The rich and poor—and not mere words,
That chicanery of knaves and fools
Is using hatreds as its tools,
That lees and larks—the streams and springs
Are essences of goodly things,
That stars upon the morning sky
Make mankind's shoddy light a lie.
When they reveal there is a God

---

[1] A paper tube through which you blew spitwads ten feet or more.

Who loves a stretch of meadow sod,
That blackbirds winging in the lea
Are far more musical than we,
That love of nature forms the art
Of linking wisdom to the heart,
It will be logic taught to live,
To tolerate and to forgive:
The skies are broad; the fields are fair;
What greater literature is there!

Droz homestead near Declo: each spring the Matthews Brothers paraded past our home on the way to Raft River bottoms.

XVIX

Farewell To Home

Here, by my hearth where the andirons gleam
And the smoke blues out like wisps of steam
I like to dream of those days so far
As the lamplight blends a distant star
Where mother with knitting by the wide hearth sat
When the kettle purred with broiling fat
As the rafters shook to the biting blast
And windowpanes were sleet o'ercast.

I take the "Bum Lamb" from the kind Basque shepherd.

God bless them all! Those friends so dear
Where we loved and we roved in the yesteryear,
   For the tide of life is a fleeting thing
   And birds have little time to sing.
Though my lines, here written, may fade to dust
   May these spoken memories ne'er be lost
   And may we fight to the end of time
That a poet may wind his fleeting rhyme.
             ...
   In honor of those who've gone before
Where the rimed lock rusts on a crumbling door,
   It is not all sadness that prompts our tears
   Who revere the friends of our distant years:
Nay! They flow from memories that shall rebound
   Wherever larks on the pastures sound,
   When a brown dog breaks the still of night,
Or the moon gleams down on the meadow white.
             ...
Sweet Elisse and Glenice with clear, bright eyes
Smile again in my hearth where the blue flames rise.
   Father is reading his paper there
Where the gray tabby curls in the cane backed chair
   (Though the sod has lain o'er him all these years,
   T'is no phantom footfall that climbs my stairs.)
   Thank God we may dream at the end of day
   In memories brighter than soul can say.

...

Though the curled board crumbles, the rose lattice falls,
I shall dream of a light in those naked halls
Of that earth-loved home by the poplared stream,
And I shall never forget to dream!
That brown dog, asleep by the mat of my door,
Reminds of the sire of sire of yore:
And swallows twittering in the eaves
Recall lost days—and fallen leaves.

Albion School.

Remembering my dad: he took our pictures, seldom was he in one of them, but this sketch fits. (Compare it with the 1913 photo on the front cover.)

My heart-felt thanks go to every reader who shared those 88 year's memories with me.

BUSTER HOUND

Ol' brown Buster hound,
I say, where did you slip off today?
Think you've been chasin' rabbits, maybe;
'Stead of stickin' around to mind the baby?
You 'gadabout', don't blink those eyes,
Lick your chops and look so wise.

You can't fool me; didn't think I'd guess
The nature of your business.
It takes *some* nerve, to appear so crazy
Scrunched by the fire, wet an' lazy,
With mud on those awkward, dirty paws
Quit lookin' sad! I'm not mad—
      not like I was!

When you came slurpin' through the kitchen
I was for broomin' ya out and pitchin'
The bones y'been savin', clean out of the yard—
But I couldn't;
You took that scolding so hard!

Now, what'cha been chasin' the rooster for?
You cornered him by the granary door;
And there's fully a dozen feathers about
Where you jerked the pride of his tail ones out!
There are plenty good reasons for you to mope;
But ya still have *some* pedigreed blood—I hope!

You lazy, old bone-diggin' fool,
Who gave you a reason to break the rule
I set for you. You can't slip out
When there's nobody else about
To watch the stock when we're short of staffin'?
But—You scalawag! I think you're laffin'—

Who 'chowsed' the colt so it broke in the hay?
You coot! O shute! Ya been BAD all day!

So listen! Brown eyes—just change your style;
Try to listen once in awhile!
You had *some* nerve to plague my rest;
Last night, you howled-it with the best
Of all the neighbor dogs I've heard.
Today, you old devil, ya won't say a word!

Sonny missed you, going to school;
Why've you been chewin' the baby's spool?
Don't try to act like a silly pup;
It's time that you start growing up!
What a sorry record for a dog your size!
Now, stop your blinkin' those wistful eyes;
We've got to correct the mistakes ya do;
You know it hurts *us*—as much as *you*?

Old Buster's name is off the rolls;
He led a noble pack.
One day, he romped a lazy knoll—
And *never* did come back!

O, if we ever meet again,
I hope we never part;
I was bigger in size,
And thought I was *wise*,
But that *dog* had the most tender heart.

Author's note: From "Poems of My Radio Days." Read over the air at Twin Falls, Nampa and Boise Stations in the late 1930s.

ONE NIGHTINGALE, ONE FROG

One day, within a sunny bog
    where April sunshine lay,
A nightingale observed a frog
    engaged in serious play.
He wore a pair of spectacles
    perched high upon his snout,
And, with a pair of calipers,
    went hopping in-and-out
Observing two fat silverfish
    he always kept about.

He carefully gauged those silverfish—
    measuring with a rule;
And, as he weighed them, he complained
    that Fate was very cruel.
A nightingale who shared the dale
    tried to stop his rant;
It flopped right over on it's back
    and wailed a weary chant,
It waved a leg, drooped a wing
    and hung its head a-slant.

The little frog broke down at last.
    Great plans had gone awry.
His puffy eyes were filled with tears;
    he gave a woeful cry:
This problem seems IMPONDERABLE—
    and that is truly sad—
He couldn't get rich without a hitch—
    only two pets he had!
(Seems he was disinherited
    when he was just a "Tad.")

Now, silverfish are insects;
    they are not fish at all;
And frogs are fond of silverfish
    as someone may recall.
No problem this;
    the "silvers" weren't forsook.
Frog studied "Raising Silverfish"
    in *Ranching By A Brook*;
So, all he needed was a lot—
    and that is where to look!

Now, here's a fact you won't refute;
    no matter if you try,
The sum of two is very small—
    and figures NEVER lie!
The silverfish looked very glum,
    not mentioned heretofore;
To offset that, they were quite fat—
    in mathematics lore—
Side-by-side, so fat and wide,
    they looked a match of four!

(This prospect grows more promising
    than data at the start,
And herein lies the miracle
    of Computation Art.)
"I've news!" chirped nightingale,
    "a way to up the count.
Those silverfish are very plump,
    increasing their amount;
It seems to me a doubled-four
    would increase like a fount!

"Where Einstein led," ol'birdie said,
    "on rockets hot in space,

Bugs would gain speed and go to seed
    in such a roomy place."
"Ay," gasped our frog so happily,
    "I never thought of this."
He planted on the birdie's beak
    a very mealy kiss.
All that nightingale could say was,
    "O, what cold remiss!"

Quoth scholar frog, "I am agog
    at what these facts implore.
Impelled in space, OUR two, by grace,
    could easily equal four!
Two, then four—set door-to-door—
    how fast they multiply;
You give and take in science law;
    you need no alibi—
Theories to make, you have to take
    a chance—and try!

"Here comes sixteen", frog said,
    "a clean, if passive, fact."
"But to proceed", warned Nightingale,
    "will take a lot of tact!
"In fact, indeed, we really need
    a different type of more;
A good slide rule, in any school,
    can net you twenty-four."
"I bow," said frog, "to what you log.
    I'm happy to the core."

"We've done it!" gasped the nightingale—
    fussing with his throat.
He downed a glass of seltzer,
    and sang the scale, en haute!

"A'ha!" he chirped. "This handy batch
    of numbers do align.
We'll stack'em all in columns—
    long zeros—and a nine!"
"Char-r-rumf!" frog concluded.
    "I say, you're doin' fine!

"S'pose I started with a hundred
    of those flaccid, flaky thugs";
Frog inquired, "Do ya'think I'd net
    a 'thousand bags' of bugs?
Well, if one half had children—
    by some odd whim of chance,
(And bugs will really do that
    if you plan it in advance.)
We'd own a carload on the hoof
    before a second glance!

"What's more," said frog, "with twenty million
    wiggling toe-to-toe,
How soon you'll get a billion
    is pretty hard to show!"
Said nightingale, "For a billion,
    ten minutes have we spent.
It follows, now, a trillion may
    have risen, grown and went—
And even one quadrillion strikes
    my crop with likely dent."

What satisfaction thinkers get
    who view the heavenly sphere
And realize they comb the depths
    of theories far and near:
Said frog, "We reached quadrillions
    without a fast re-wind;

I'm satisfied and I suspect
    our facts are well combined."
"It's possible", said nightingale,
    "we left a few behind."
The frog lay down and flexed his thighs
    upon a sunny rock.
The sky was clear and azure
    as bees buzzed 'round the block.
The nightingale began to rise
    and squinted at the sun.
"This math," he said, "is E-Z
    when you get off number one!
And now, I think I'll gather worms."
    With that he was gone.

When but a lad, confined with mumps,
    I spent time out of school.
For once, I thought a little while
    and penned this simple rule:
A stupid oaf, by striving hard,
    may pontificate and drool;
But only raving idiots
    will match wits with a fool!

HARD TIMES
PART I
INFLUENZA

In the winter of 1918-19 there was a major epidemic in the aftermath of World War 1. Albion was isolated by canyon roads, hampered by snow and ice. So many were down with flu, there were scarcely enough people on their feet to tend the sick. Albion cemetery bears dated testaments to the host of young and old who died that winter.

In Declo, my mother, Olga H. Droz, was constantly asked to attend the sick, but no one in our family became ill. Forest F. Bauer in his memoirs describes the epidemic of 1918. He reports it took many lives and nearly everyone in the city had a siege of it. "My mother," he wrote, "never recovered from it and passed away in 1919."

I remember Olga Droz's disappointment when she took me with her that last visitation to the Bauer Building. Yes, I was along that day. Fortunately none of us contacted the flu. There was so little anyone could do. The illness developed rapidly and results were often fatal.

I remember another tragedy. One of the Thorne family wrote as follows: "Everything seemed to be going fine until the winter of 1918-1919. The flu bug hit Declo. All nine of the Thorne family were down at least once. We couldn't get anyone to come, as everyone had the flu. The Parke boys came to take care of our stock and milk the cow. We all survived, except our Mother, Adelia, who died January 5, 1919 at the age of thirty-eight. Not only our family, but many families suffered deep sorrow at this time."

Declo State Bank was an unusually handsome

red-brick, one story building on a corner of Main Street. The sidewalk that fronted the east and north ended as abruptly as the last brick of its ostentatious façade, bordered by Joe Walker's orchard. It was started in 1917, but it's life as a bank was short lived. It closed somewhere between the years of 1920-21.

That's one time my father, Robert H. Droz, came home in tears. I'd never seen him cry before. Our income from harvest was in that bank, the whole year's profits. Now our nest egg was gone.

We entered a time of hardscrabble living tempered with pride, and what a ride. Hard times settled in like a plague of pillaging crows after Declo bank failed. In years that followed we ground along (spring, summer and fall) when a son's pay for helping on the farm all week was a couple of dollars, which bought necessities and a six-bit movie on Saturday night. I felt lucky to get an overcoat for winter, a pair of boots, some new underwear and socks. We had a straw mattress on my bed, and a feather tick over us; yet we weren't poor in my mind.

PART II

LORENZO

Lorenzo Oliver came to Cassia County around 1909 from Iowa. He had been a brakeman on the railroad but wanted to try his hand at farming; so he settled half a mile from our door.

Slight of build, stooped and thin from erosion of life, he was unfortunate because he had no son to carry his family name or help work the farm. There were five women in Lorenzo's household so he missed male companionship. He came to our house on long and lonely winter evenings after chores to rock-and-talk with father. They shared joys and miseries together

while my dad puffed a pipe and stoked the stove.
Lorenzo was a gentle, mild and friendly man we liked immensely. His hands told by their gnarled, knobby look he was accustomed to toil and further disclosed he had arthritis. He favored a persistent habit of snapping his knuckles after getting comfortable by the fire.
His face was Irish for sure, his visage kind and sad. He loved to recall the old days. Father was of a similar mind; so they got along very well. Lorenzo often mentioned his childhood. Here's one incident he recounted I shall never forget. I hope his departed spirit forgives me for changing the original dialog since I cannot recapture fully the excellence he displayed on reciting these stories. That was a long time ago, but the vital points are true.
"One winter," Lorenzo began," when I was a small boy in Iowa, a specific incident stood out sharply from all the rest; it left a scar on my life!" He stopped and studied our faces.
Father always encouraged this old neighbor to talk things out. For he knew Lorenzo was lonely and discouraged, delving the past does seem to be good medicine. Dad led him on by asking questions and adding his own observations to help Lorenzo unwind.
"What happened that year that was so unusual?" he inquired.
Lorenzo liked to weigh every word. "Well, Robert, you and I have seen plenty of hardship but that one beat all records. Remember, now; I was just a boy." He pondered a time, staring at the darkness through a slit in the curtains. The wind had risen and poplars moaned by the gate.
We settled in our chairs wondering what would come. That little man could be mischievous. He loved to keep you guessing.

"That year started out better than most," he continued, pleased with attentive friends. "We had a nice stand of corn and the sows had full litters; so papa was thankful; but, when harvest was over, the price of corn fell because of surplus. Next, the price of hogs dropped to where it didn't pay to feed 'em." He leaned back and cracked his knuckles in agitation. We wanted him to go on, but he just sat there with a far away look.

"Come on, Lorenzo, finish the story," said my dad.

"What happened was plain enough; we had to tighten our belts and get set for hard times, and we did. My father was strict."

"Yes, the old timers were strict," father chimed in. "Once, back in Lignières, I proved I didn't deserve a licking my dad gave me. That big Swiss, a powerful man, only laughed and said, 'Well, charge it off to times you deserved one and didn't get caught'!"

Both men laughed. Lorenzo continued. "My father was careful with everything including clothes. He had many mouths to feed and cut expenses to the bone. When harvest was over, he bought each of us a pair of shoes."

"To last the whole year?" father queried. "Nothing else?"

'Yes, that was it—one pair apiece, and I was hard on shoes like any kid that's growing too fast. Worst of all, I was careless and lost one. I don't remember how it happened."

We listened in silence. "Maybe the pup ran off with it," dad volunteered.

"I don't rightly know, but I got a thrashing for being careless; then came the first snow."

"What did you do?"

"Well," Lorenzo observed, "You'll think I'm lyin' if I tell the rest."

"No, I won't, tell us about it."

"All right. I kept walking to school and helped with farm chores. I brought in wood, sometimes, and did lots of other tasks the best way I could, but it was hard to manage that foot without a shoe." The lamp flickered; we sat very still in the shadows. Dad broke the silence.

"Did someone take pity and buy you another?" he asked hopefully.

"No such luck!" Lorenzo muttered and snapped his knuckles one final time.

"First, I put on a woolen sock; then, I wrapped my foot the best I could with a gunnysack before I went outside; that was all I could think to do."

We stared at him in awe, sorry for the small figure huddled there in the big rocker.

"I sure had a time to keep it from freezing," he continued. Every eye centered on his face.

'The snow was deep that year, and it was bitter cold."

"I just don't see how you managed!" dad exclaimed.

"It *was* difficult," Lorenzo agreed. "Seemed like bad weather would never end. I hopped along, anyway, hoping, somebody would cut a trail for me; and I clumped around with only one shoe that entire winter."

"Good gosh!" father cried. "Those *were* hard times!"

Pop's orders wuz:
"Slop the hogs,
pick up the mail,
no shoes or not –
and do not fail!"

PART III
HARD TIMES? TOP THESE!

This report is so well told, I see no point in much rephrasing an episode from *Declo, My Town, My People* that proves the ingenuity of two men I knew way back when. They once were our neighbors a scant few miles away.

A couple of fellows from Declo, Bill Jibson and Melvin Doman, owned a Model T Ford. Now this car had a problem, it had a flat crankshaft and because of this, they could not keep bearings in it. So they resorted to the simple expedient of using bacon rind for bearing material! That's right, no kidding!

In those days money was almost non-existent and to get a new crankshaft was out of the question as was the possibility of getting a new car. So, they dropped the oil pan off, as often as necessary, and wrapped bacon rind around the crankshaft to take up the slack. The old car then carried them back and forth to work for two or three weeks before it was necessary to replace the bacon rind.

Both men were mechanics, working for a construction firm, and the repair of these bearings on their car had to be done so many times that they could team up on it and have it done in about two hours.

It was such a common occurrence, in fact, that it became a standing joke between them. When they were going to drive some place one would say,

"You go and shave while I take up the bearings, then we'll be on our way." And who said those were the "good old days?"

Dr. Olga Louise Droz and family at St. Anthony, ID, 1913. The author is perched on his father's shoulder.

Patriotic post cards from France – World War I.

63

THE COTTEREL BRIDE

Chapter I

The Courting

The Union Pacific train puffed into Burley one sunny morning a long time ago.[1] The porter brought a stool, and out stepped a girl from Alsace-Lorraine and a city no one recalls. If that young lady had spotted what lay ahead as she stepped on the clay of Idaho, I wonder would she have been so eager to be "pitched in the briar patch" of Uncle Remus with a million other rabbits?

Having lived among the knolls of Cotterel where this girl was headed, the one telling this tale remembers these things well. There, we strained our wits for naught and nearly wound up brittle, brown mummies in that desert debacle, standing with dry throats over a vast, invisible water reservoir no one knew existed. What a grim twist that was!

Many old timers collaborated on a history of those times. *Declo, My Town, My People* referred to some of the trials we met. One pioneer west of Cotterel reported that rabbits pouring off the desert were so thick at the edge of Snake River there wasn't room to add another whisker, all were jostling for sips. The man's family boiled the water bailed from that point.

Draught took continual toll; grasshoppers burgeoned in clouds of blurring wings, devouring everything their choppers could rip.

If younger readers tire of my complaints about dry farming, I'll say this: historians, in 1996, as I compose this memoir, have updated concerns to record. They will decry the ravage of AIDS, the exorbitant cost of a home. They will pen new chapters on inflation,

---

[1] Year 1914 is about right to begin this true tale. Many names have been changed to protect descendants.

rising medical costs, and the exploding fees of a college education. Let each generation write the record as they should; let me deal with the period between 1910 and 1920—and with Cotterel.

This is a tale of two brothers and one bride. I'm going to call the girl at the opening of this account Maurine. There are two brothers she expected to meet this day. Name one Johann, the other Wilhelm.

None of these names are real, but the people were real enough. As a boy, I stored butterflies in envelopes with naphthalene flakes to preserve them. The naphtha dissipated; tiny predators bored in. Dissected portions of clouded sulfur and skipper butterflies lay in the crease of a wrapper. Most names, dates and places captured were intact. Wings might be shattered, but colorful scales, even patterns survived. Tracking settlers requires related techniques. You build a picture from fragments hidden so long. You search records, memories, whispers and echoes; people emerge.

There she is! There's Maurine at Burley station, waiting for a carriage. She has no conception of events ahead. Can't someone tell her? "Girl, beware! Your destiny will tilt in the flick of a lash. Ahead of you lie days of heat, harsh winds and rattling collisions with Fate. War will erupt soon! Be on guard!" No use; she will not hear. You're speaking to a hologram locked in the long ago—the "dreamtime."

That's what memories are, frozen holograms. The people moved on; some are dead. Like the song about The Girl From Ipanema: "...she doesn't see!" Her eyes have settled on poplar leaves twinkling by the tracks on a promising day! Pretend we snap our fingers to stir that China doll. Wake her now!

Johann came striding up. "Welcome to America!" he said with a bow. They embraced as his

65

lips pecked her cheek for an instant. They'd simply been casual friends in the homeland until lonely letters from a classmate convinced this maid to cross an ocean; *pens pack power.* At this point of the story, details slipped away.

    I contacted my sisters in Santa Monica, asking for clues. "May graduated from Declo Grade School," Dora began. "I'd skipped upward, a grade or so, and wasn't far behind her. Burley was ten miles away. They had a high school there. For two months, May and I stayed with the lady we've labeled Maurine. She'd left Cotterel to live in Burley by then. Did you know she'd emigrated from Alsace-Lorraine? That unfortunate country had been annexed by Germany years before. Maurine had honey-blonde hair and winning ways."

    "What else do you remember?" I asked.

    "For one thing, she was full of good humor. She loved to sing "*La Marseillaise.*" How she rolled the R's on *patrie, gloire* and *arrivé* when she belted it.

    "We enjoyed listening to her unique brand of French. She was also quite fluent in German. That German enunciation collided with her French dialect, unusual sounds to our Swiss heritage. When Maurine tried to speak English, her hybrid 'dialog' sounded stranger still: it's now a melange with overtones of English, French and German; and that's about enough for one little immigrant to handle. We were careful not to snicker, for we loved her. Maurine made a bed in the front room, each night, tucking us in so tenderly. Perhaps she was extra kind because of the unstinting care mother gave her years before. Maurine was generous and tidy, too. If the house had been larger, she'd have kept us for the whole term. In time, mother, found other lodgings, but we missed our friend."

    A world war was under way in Europe at the

very time immigrants were pouring into Cassia County, Idaho. Some headed for Cotterel dry lands. Others sought irrigable tracts. It was a hectic time. The glow-

New settlers arriving in Burley

From the *Burely Bulletin*, June 28, 1914. (Special thanks to Verna Anderson, Advertising Director, and Ann Harper, Business Manager, Burley South Idaho Press, for assisting with newspaper archives from which this and the following photos were copied.)

ing optimism of the day was best expressed in the statement that "acres of land are available...growing nothing but worthless sagebrush and destructive jackrabbits, merely from a lack of people to farm it." On the same page as the above photo is a picture of the Grand Duke of Tuscany displaying a perfect handlebar mustache. He sports a short-billed officer's cap full of braid and glory with three stars *shining* on the collar of his coat. Caption reads: "The grand duke of Tuscany is commander of the Austrian forces that were sent into Alsace to assist the Germans."

GRAND DUKE OF TUSCANY

Maurine may have embarked for America around the spring of 1914, arriving at Burley close to the week the world blew apart. In this vein, she was lucky to depart just then. Archduke Ferdinand was assassinated at Sarajevo, on June 28, 1914, precipitating a holocaust like none before it.

"Franz Josef has been called the emperor of sorrow. The 'curse of the Hapsburgs' is said by the superstitious to have followed his kin. The 'curse' was pronounced by the aged Countess Carolyn, whose son was put to death for participating in the Hungarian uprising. She called upon heaven and hell to blast the happiness of Franz Josef and strike him 'through those he loved'. Thus he has been stricken...." (*Burley Bulletin*, 28 June 1914.)

Maurine, like a majority of Alsace-Lorrainians, disliked being Germany's puppet. Recall, as Dora mentioned, Maurine sang *La Marseillaise* with vigor (after WW I) when my sisters lived with Maurine a short time? It's easy to see she sang that song to celebrate restoration of Alsace-Lorraine to France in 1919. The homeland was free, and she was free in America. Twice blessed! Isn't it strange how random snippets lock together? "March on, our day of Glory arrives!" verse one of *La Marseillaise* proclaims.

If you're still reading, in spite of my digressions, we'll go back to that couple we left dangling at the station while we gathered more facts about them. Johann is loading Maurine's luggage on a four wheel rig. She's a winsome sight, sitting in the carriage, ready for a spin. It should be easy for her to catch our rhythm and match our step. The "Melting Pot" is briskly bubbling in Burley.

The team clips along; the sun is bright. What a wonderful day to chatter about a wedding. The narrow rims and "spidery" spokes of the "canvas-topper" sparkle and spin. Maurine's escort tells her of a "Little Gray Home less than twenty miles away."

"What's it like?" she wonders aloud.

"Well, there's lamp light to read by, a rocker to rest in and lots more," he replies. If you're a poet, that sounds cozy—ignoring all the chores that come with a cabin. Wood to cut, water to fetch.

Now let's change the tense and the mood: Three hundred twenty acres of land to clear was not rosy, or easy to dwell your fancy on. The cabin was teeny, and it certainly was gray out there!

That scraggly brush hard by the door, jackrabbits rambling down bouldered gullies, brought no poetic triumph. Wandering clouds scudding across Heglar knolls spread pendulous shadows, weaving blindly across dunes and rocky batholiths, like hoboes searching for a grubstake.

There's a pall of gray across the sun when hot winds rollick, plucking tubs of dust to loft them over neighbor's digs; a friendly gesture indeed! There Johann and, sometimes Will, who spent more time in town, battled the barrens, riding bucking-rails, tearing out brush roots—everything was dry as powdered peat!

Enough of that prologue. Let's return to Burley, a fine city for that day. Maurine is enchanted by thoughts of great adventures in the western setting of a wonderful place called Idaho. Johann proudly heads southward from Burley depot on the very-main street of that farming town with a dazzling girl beside him.

First big building they passed was a grain elevator. Next came a bank to impress the richest, embarrass or scare the poorest. This portion of town boasted a corner where farmers, "gapers" and loungers often leaned or perched, until the bank put spikes on a railing; some laggards had no mind to budge until late-night spots opened. It was a gathering place where farmers met and greeted friends. Rupert's park, nine miles distant, had a square and bandstand crossing, also a meeting place for friends—you got a feeling the country and city had joined hands and initiated a truce, such a good idea.

By this prestigious bank corner rattled buggies and hayracks stacked with household goods—as well as mom, "gram'pa" and the kids—of incoming Europeans pulled by animated, light-stepping horses. How their clattering hooves improved Burley's frontier impact, live as a Pickwickian scroll—and I was there!

Autos were rare, but there were a few—like the majestic Hayne's automobile, a modern marvel of the time. BUY AMERICA'S GREATEST "LIGHT SIX," only $1485.

The result of 22 years' successful experience in building motor cars

BURLEY BULLETIN June 28, 1914

America's Greatest "Light Six" $1485

A "Light Six" That's Different

The Studebaker Company wasn't building cars then. Our Studebaker was a wagon (choke less—and smokeless). A few cheap jitneys came rolling with a "Pucka! Pucka! Winnemucca!" Draft animals were our support in the outback.; you could mire a jitney there. Small towns of America, how grand you were—when hitching rails were common everywhere, and weedy lots hosted polyglot rigs, with horses drowsing, stomping and whinnying by turns, gigged to the side board of a wagon, glad for the rest.

Every town had livery stables where spirits of ammonia and aromatic Lucerne hay bales commingled with rarer stuff. A whiff of kerosene was one treat that wrinkled your nostrils, spreading from a battered can with a dollop of candy that a grocer stuck on the spout. Children's olfactory glands are potent and tolerant. I didn't mind the smell of those little green buns the horses laid along our course with no shame; they were fresh and pungent. Best of all, we loved the richness of spices and oranges. Who could ever forget those bakery smells—M-m-m! There were so many treasures and pleasures in that bustling city by the Snake.

Blacksmith hammers rang. Clamors of commerce kept schoolboy's eyes rolling, especially kids from the hills. Before our youth departed and adult senses were dulled by time, cities were exciting. Following old foot steps, down sidewalks we skipped on, seventy-five-years ago. (Now, pale forms, and soft echoes, like a doleful wind, fill the eaves of my mind.)

Johann and Maurine reviewed such scenes. She looks very pert in a bonnet filled with ribbons and bows. Johann and this lovely European have toured the town. Now their carriage spins back down Overland Avenue. Its time to meet the third actor in the play, named Wilhelm.

That worthy "mover" is searching for yard goods, curtains and oil cloth. Johann just dropped him off the rig on his jaunt to the depot. It was a blithe and bonny morn when they drove here from Cotterel; but the noon is nighing. Those two wary bachelors, at this point, knew they needed something colorful, lacy and un-male to decorate that dismal, tar-papered cabin in the sage, dreading the moment their crude, gate-hinged door swung open, and that beautiful guest from European halls met plain-vanilla disaster.

The outside view was primitive too! You could say the plumbing was of "Standard Brand"—a board-battened nineteen-fourteen-model no less!—commonly called a "two-holer" that never gets flushed, or embarrassed. Once every two years, on schedule, you push it over, fill the hole, and move it ten feet. There is an enormous potential for relocation when you have 320 acres to aim at. You will be gone before there's no place remaining to park it. That's some consolation for a cold seat, don't you agree?

Other shortcomings of the mansion and grounds you'll hear about soon enough. Johann was optimistic, viewing all that land, thinking how a girl in gingham would light up his digs. Romantic visions make unpainted walls change to magic halls when the wick's turned low and shadows flicker by a crackling stove. This was his recurring dream, and on it goes.

A simple cabin assumes new dimensions when you burst in, hungry and cold, to be kissed-and-greeted with hot supper—taters'n-gravy, baked ham, biscuits, home churned butter and apple pie. The fire makes it bloom even more, but a kind-hearted woman, knitting by the hearth, makes a cracker-box seem a castle. You lie in an easy chair. Let the weary wind rave and batter the pane. You're home!

The clock ticks cheerfully. There's no tomorrow; this night is forever. An old fashioned Victorola plays a Strauss waltz; you fall asleep. The dream stops here.

The two, with wedding plans in tow, chattered a storm. Johann tied the team behind a Golden Rule Store. The atmosphere was as wholesome as it sounds. Mercantile stores had a human touch.

They shopped together for the first time. Johann missed the "Old Country." It was good to hear news of home, sharing the best days of your life with a priceless companion of such grace and beauty.

He thought of all the interests they shared in common. As for Maurine, she was pleased with his good manners and wholesome looks. Johann felt a tingle when her arm brushed his. Others who passed them glanced at this miss with admiration in a land where women were scarce enough, and pretty ones were jewels.

"Wilhelm has to be around here, someplace," Johann ventured, coming out of a trance. Maurine searched the crowd.

Was he anything like the mischievous, young man she faintly remembered, whom the girls often made such a fuss over?

He'd paid little attention to her, back in Europe. They had attended the same school. Perhaps he thought her immature. Now, she realized their difference of age was unimportant; her heart skipped deliciously. I once had a crush on Will, she thought; but then, I was silly and younger. She straightened the pin in her hat used to tame those golden braids in the Idaho wind.

What a beautiful woman; what a grand day!

But she was to marry Johann. Time to be resolute. That's what she decided.

"This is where Will said he'd meet us," Johann opined as they strolled arm in arm.

A stocky man waved from the opposite curb. "Hel-lo-o-o! I'll be right over!" Apt to scowl if he didn't like you, more volatile than his brother, this newcomer exuded maturity and confidence, automatically sensing what to say on any occasion. He gave that blushing girl a rousing hug. Wilhelm, a man endowed with special charms, sensed Maurine was vulnerable to him.

Shopping concluded, the three chatterers spun out of Burley at a trotter's clip, with a stocky man manning the team handily, just the way he ran everything else. Maurine and Johann swayed in the back patent leather seat as fences rippled by.

Wilhelm planned a spirited dialog to keep the action moving. When they'd trotted less than a mile, he pointed his whip at a glade by the river.

"There's a fine picnic spot; we'll stop there, next time we come into town."

He could manage anything, a business love affair or fight, I suppose.

Those passengers had small chance to discuss Maurine's recent trip or make wedding-bell plans. Will kept interrupting; he certainly knew how to entertain a woman. The wheels rolled past Unity curve; cressy rivulets sparkled at Springdale, but scenery wasn't important to him. Will's dialog gunned right along as two puffing horses splay-tracked for Marshfield.

We call it Declo now. There, Lar Gillette managed Frank Clark's grocery in 1913 or 1914. It became J. C. Murphy's Mercantile years later.

They didn't even stop at Marshfield. Dominating Will abandoned the blue-green fields of Minidoka Irrigation Project in a trice.

There lay the desert! Russian thistles hemmed the track, a rude shock for Maurine. What scenery she enjoyed was a mass of juniper foothills on the south, but the road they followed was headed for *desolation*. Wilhelm stopped the buggy before they reached the edge of Dewey Ranch. He handed the binoculars to Maurine and pointed at a landmark forever fixed in every Cotterel-dweller's mind.

"Look, there's a jump-off spot of rock called 'the Point'; it's the northernmost tip of Cotterel Mountain. Emigrant trails converge near here. Thousands of wagons passed by from 1843 to 1869. Then, a continental railroad ended their trek. Some of the Old Oregon trail ruts, two or three sets, side by side, are still visible."

Our be-ribboned immigrant was impressed. Some people know how to make every hill an adventure. They fill every bare plain with buffaloes, Indians riding bareback, and ancient legends.

The three looped around the point of the mountain. There was Cotterel. It was Sam Cotterel's town, Sam Cotterel's dream

The buggy rolled merrily on.

Then Will stopped again. "Over there," he said, "is the homestead." Although Johann and Will were partners in this venture, everything Johann had done, including raising the cabin and clearing the land, seemed to shrink away. He pondered this point. It seemed Wilhelm took a lot of credit for success of ventures they shared, but "J" was not contentious. He felt little need to prove himself.

A German family, one of several in Cotterel, volunteered room and board for Maurine until a wedding date was set. Johann went to visit her nearly every evening. In that busy time, both brothers were clearing their home site, putting up curtains, doing beaver's tasks that settlers do. At this stage Wilhelm was very helpful, adding cupboards and shelves to the cabin.

After all, "J" was the one getting married, wasn't he? So, this was a favor to him, wasn't it? Staying with the neighbors, visiting the homestead from time to time, Maurine was beginning to have misgivings as they talked of the wedding. She knew she should be radiantly happy, but couldn't forget Will. Am I fickle? she wondered, feeling the guilt.

After all, Johann had paid her fare. Her head advised her to honor a vow; her heart disagreed. Will, sly fellow, saw this maiden in a different light there on the homestead. Pretty girls were scarce in a land of bachelors.

Maybe Will tried to avoid stealing his brother's choice. No one will ever know.

Meanwhile, the partners kept railing brush, piling rocks, preparing land to plant, digging holes for miles of fence. Juniper posts had to be cut and hauled from the mountain top; the list of needs went on and on. Johann visited his idol faithfully, but plans can go wrong by a shift of breeze. Wilhelm made a few visits of his own, stopping for a casual chat with you know who.

This was just good manners, wasn't it? He

didn't have to play the role of "mooning lover;" competition never worried that lad.

He told Maurine what a jewel she was; he wasn't bashful or hesitant, not him. They fell in love, and that was it. This incident peeves me a bit for a reason you should know. Wilhelm was the "older brother," and older brothers have a knack. I had two older brothers. They'll "do-you-in" on short notice! Wilhelm may have disliked piracy; but he didn't quit.

When the bride-to-be made a final choice, how could she break the news to the loser? How would he react? She pondered this on a particular evening as Johann climbed the grade to her gate.

"Good evening! Come, walk with me."

It was a cool evening, appreciated on the desert. A planet gleamed; the moon drifted through tufts of cloud; nighthawks wove and swooped above. Those booming wings made pleasing interludes. It was a lover's night, but something was amiss.

Johann must have realized, that his brother was smitten. America is a free country; I think he expected the ax to fall—clean, sharp and to the point.

"I'm so sorry, Johann! I do not love you, though I admire you a lot! It is hard to say this, but I must!" She paused to note his reaction, searching for words. "You may have noticed—I've changed!"

"I love your brother. Forgive me if I hurt you. I never planned this." Her distress was plain.

In spite of his nagging suspicions, Johann was desolate—his life torn apart. Love crumbled away. He looked up at the grim profile of rim-rock capping the mountain, forever anchored. He, like this radiant maid, was trapped by the heart's urge, such a long way from home—such a big change ahead. After a time he took her hand and said: "I was blind—should have guessed! I kept hoping small things I noticed weren't true."

They talked a long time; he would always bear scars of this fatal disappointment, but no harsh recriminations arose. Months of strain that followed proved he wore no grudge. Such unselfishness is hard to find.

Chapter II
When Wedding Bells Cease Ringing

Maurine and Wilhelm were married. The wedding was a happy affair with no fancy trimmings. The honeymoon was far too brief, I suspect. Each of us in that dismal-dryland was caught in a lion's claws. There was precious little time to celebrate at Cotterel.

Not long after Wilhelm and Maurine married, those two brothers bought a car. With this added mobility, Wilhelm continued working on the irrigation project. New land involves so much effort and capital. You must buy lumber, hardware, hay, and seed. The list goes on and on. If you didn't watch, that wolf, snuffing 'round the door, gets braver. Each morning Wilhelm rose early and headed off for the project. He could do this because his brother was always there to help around the homestead.

A year drifted by. In the hottest days of summer, a man rode to our homestead asking for a doctor. You could suppose that meant my dad was the one he sought. Not so! Mother was the doctor at our house, trained in Geneva, Switzerland. She was licensed for General Practice, but her specialty was Obstetrics.

She started practice at Lignières; then she crossed an ocean like so many Europeans of that time. Mother had an extensive practice in Cotterel.

The man asking for help that day, was no other than tender hearted Johann. He didn't waste time.

"Mrs. Droz, Maurine's having a baby. She has hard pains; they're happening often! Will you come?"

Dad hooked up our rig and placed me in it. He couldn't leave the farm. Mama grabbed her satchel and assorted instruments, shooing my sisters along the path toward the team. She certainly had a handful to manage.

My sisters think it was five miles or more through rough terrain to the patient's homestead. Mother clucked to the team, and we headed out at a spanking trot.

Driving from our house at Cotterel to that secluded homestead of the bride from Alsace-Lorraine, I'll reconstruct the jaunt from rides I took in the same buggy on desert roads, years afterward. Our conveyance was once a two-seater; then, one seat was removed to accommodate loose cargo. My sisters sat on the floor, in the back end, watching ruts ripple and waver beneath their feet. Riding backwards in a buggy was great fun! You could term this framework a buckboard, but we called it "The Buggy." It had the advantages of an open-air car, and even more thrills.

There was the rich fume of desert sage without carbon monoxide, the caress of a cool breeze that rippled hair ribbons and met, head on, with fascinating whirligigs that danced across the headland like wayward sprites. We had unlimited view with no windshield obstructions. Our gait was leisurely and offered little danger to life or limb.

You could actually jump off without fear and run behind the rig when the horses slowed to a walk. You could pick a wild flower and clamber aboard without a driver caring.

And so it went: all of us have a bouncing good time; up through ruts and rocks mother wove; one more bend and we're at the cabin.

Mother tied the team in high brush, cautioning two maids in pigtails to watch for rattlers and scorpions. Mother wasn't afraid to leave them in charge of that small child on a blanket spread in what shade existed. Young as they were, they watched me without complaining. Babies are always a problem. When I fell asleep, the girls played in the rocks at games ranging from Indian raids to a fancy tea.

Dr. Droz, carrying a black case full of remedies, hurried up-trail wondering how near to delivery her patient was. Entering the cabin, she was struck by the primitive accommodations. The patient looked worn and discouraged. There was no one present except Johann, relieved help arrived so quickly.

What would this couple have accomplished without Johann's aid? He became nurse, cook and servant, even before the baby arrived. That fine young man wouldn't abandon the only kin he had; that was his strength.

He brought mother whatever she called for during delivery, he was faithful as a rock that endures in the gale.

On mother's second visit she grew concerned about the new infant who had cried a lot during the night, although the men had done their best to calm him. Johann, in particular, was concerned for his tiny nephew.

Mother bathed it. She often used flaxseed rinses for common skin eruptions, but I don't know what she did for problems as bad as this one. If she couldn't calm the infection, that baby would die—but she was determined.

Into the black satchel she pries. I'll never forget that array of glass tubes, each in a special slot. Her portable pharmacy's well stocked; how often she brought it to my sick bed.

Mother made a last check of the infant, sleeping at last, then returned to that worried form on a pipe-framed bed so much in need of care and comfort. Several things bonded Mother and Maurine, for a lifetime: they both spoke French; both were immigrants. They'd cut all ties, except for letters, lamenting the void that could never be filled.

Mother gave Johann full instructions on caring for the two invalids. He must have been well-trained in *somebody's* kitchen, she decided with a thankful heart.

"I'll be back in the morning," mama said. "Good night, dear! You'll be all right!"

Dr. Droz climbed in the buggy, her brood intact, and rattled home.

Chapter III

A Cabin In the Sage

On the next visit, one of a series of trips mother made to that isolated cabin, she brought necessities for the fretting mother and ailing infant. Among these blessings was a bolt of netting to fend off flies, those black vagrants more troublesome than the worst whining mosquitoes. She arranged netting over Maurine's bed and baby's crib. She handed Johann more of it to tack over windows. How could anyone manage without screens? Mother lifted that woebegone patient's head and fed her like a daughter, speaking in French, the language they loved.

Maurine retained the broth. It was clear her fever had lowered; the medication mother prescribed was effective. Now, came a sponge bath. Imagine, the only water on site was in a keg outside. The partners had to haul it from the well or from Cotterel spring, tepid but potable.

Some farms had cisterns that kept the water cool

for a time. Auxiliary barrels placed topside gave the water a woody taste. We never needed to find a gas station at the bend. We were alone in a pristine environment, watching the clouded sulfur butterfly, or a veined white one, titillate on a warm breeze. Sad it is you can no longer find such primitive scenes.

> There, the sundial-dandelion
> Lifts a hoary-headed scion
> Among flagellant, buttery fellows
> Decked in bright arrays of yellows,
> Gathered near the dragonflies
> With their multifidous eyes!

Another visit to that cabin in the sage. Mother clucked to the team. Each time we left, father watched us cross the road and head toward the roughest scrub land southeast of our homestead. He was working from dawn to dusk and didn't have any fat left. Mom took some of us with her so father could work.

This day he climbed back on the roof of a two story wood-frame and resumed his rhythmic rite. First, he slapped down a shingle; then sank two blue nails to lock it tight. "Tap! Tap!" then a pause. "Tap! Tap!" went the hammer again, a pleasant, familiar sound.

Dad would stop, now and then, to trace the dust cloud we trailed, until the entourage vanished behind a batholith. Heat waves flickered across the foothills. "That's no decent place for greenhorns to settle," father grumbled to Roy, who was helping on the roof. A breeze out of nowhere tried to snatch a shingle from the stack beside them.

Dad had come to the U.S., much earlier than mother. He emigrated from Lignières in the canton of Neuchatel, Switzerland on March 16, 1892; both dad and mother hailed from that place. Father became accustomed to American ways, though the language was a trial for his tongue. Once, Dad returned to Switzerland, in 1902, to visit the old mill where he'd ground wheat during the day and sawed lumber at night.

My father's pa-pa was not always fair; it made little difference to him that working until midnight caused his son to fall asleep during school. From this experience my father learned life's hard lessons and the miller's trade as well. After years of "barnstorming" on a host of adventures across the U.S. and all the way to the Yukon, he returned home to Switzerland for one final visit with family and friends. It was then he courted a classmate, Olga Descombés. They married September 26, 1902, and sailed for America a month later. Date of embarkation from Le Havre was October 26, 1902. They would never see Switzerland again.

There was a town on the prairie called Neuchatel, Kansas where a Swiss colony rooted, a haven for French-speaking arrivals after learning the "ropes." Dad had made friends there in the ten restless years of his bachelorhood. He tried many ventures that failed, like the time he bought Arkansas land "sight-unseen" from a land shark—only to discover it was swampland. Father traveled from Eastern climes all the way to Seattle to join the Klondike; it was a groaning morass climbing Chilkoot Pass—but let's get back to the "Lower Forty-eight."

Perhaps father's connections with folks at Neuchatel, Kansas, were helpful in getting him an excellent position. Based on old experience, he became the manager of a Roller Mill in Centralia, Kansas, but mill dust was his undoing. He developed a cough that plagued his life.

Mother sent him to a specialist who said: "Quit the mill or die young!"

I'm sure mother had felt protected because of

dad's firm entrenchment in the profitable milling industry. She'd planned to drop medical practice if family duties required it. Now, all that future collapsed. Giving up that Roller Mill not only disappointed my parents; it was a tragedy for all of us

Father could work as a carpenter, or he could install new mills as a millwright before they started production, but his health was always at risk. He still had adventure in his veins; so he traveled west to St. Anthony, Idaho, where he built a home. Some millwrights can be carpenters without much ado. The newspaper columns were full of news; there was free land in Cotterel!

Granaries were full there, newspapers reported. Father sold a home he'd just built in St. Anthony, Idaho. From some of the proceeds he bought our Studebaker wagon, put on wooden bows and canvas. Presto, we were the last of the pioneers heading for Cotterel and great wealth. In truth we wound up stranded on a grim patch of dry land. No matter how many times I report this, it somehow seems like new news; you'll find this continual refrain in all the memoirs Cotterelites ever write.

Father tucked a fistful of blue nails in the corner of his cheek and adjusted the shingle into line, running nigh-to-five inches to-the-weather per the gauge of his hatchet. (It varied from four and one half inches to the maximum of five. The more left to the weather, the less the shingles lasted. I must admit we crowded the gauge a bit. It took less shingles for a job.)

The wind was up; there might be rain and the roof had to go on. That is what dad figured at the time, but the truth is it seldom rained. As we said so many times, "Rain doesn't follow the plow," despite bogus claims to the opposite from real-estate speculators. What a land salesman's petard that was! More fools us!

Back to mother's doctoring. The buckboard slowed to a slack-rein crawl as mom's buggy team minced over sharp-edged boulders some wagon wheel had fractured. Stones anchored in dry ruts were hard on the tender feet of Snuke and Cheyenne—the latter, a mare from Wyoming, sported a wine cup brand. It was an attractive design. (If one has to be burned it might as well be an elegant "license plate.") Both were unshod. Blacksmiths were far away and shoes cost money.

The sandy soil was generally kind, but this was "last choice" terrain. The girls sniffed the sagy air. Pungent rabbit brush glowed in hollows: those yellow-pastel florets were welcome after dull earth tones and smoky-brushed coulees.

It seemed unbearably hot, but my sisters didn't mind. Mother parked the team in the best shade available. This was a forest of sagebrush and cactus buttons.

Three of us would have disrupted that cabin. Mother gave my sisters a pep talk as they took me in tow. She left us there to play in the sage once more. I'm relegated to the blanket like poor Linus in a Peanuts comic—a trial to manage is my guess.

There was not a shade tree in sight; the place simply sizzled. Can you realize what a chore this was for mother. She had enough problems and cares just tending her own home. There were five children to cook, wash and mend for, and don't forget a husband expecting good Swiss cuisine three times a day. On each trip to that lonely shack, we went through the same routine as mother followed the dusty track to visit a lonely woman who needed company as much as medicine.

Mother and Maurine shared a good chat; how

the French declensions flowed. Now the doctor lifts the wiggly-pygmy from his basket and uncurls a bandage. Voila!

"Maurine, he's better today," she says with a smile. "You're baby's going to be fine!"

Mother loved tikes. Obstetrics was the right choice for her career. She bathed'im, powdered'im, and put on a new bandage. She rocked him a while, and then she sang a Swiss lullaby:

Mon petite lapin,   *Ne cours plus*
As tu du chagrin?   *Dans le jardin,*
Tu ne sautes plus,   *Din, din, din, din!*

My wife insists mothers sing to babies when small, for they can hear. That song was out of the old time in a land of chalets and high peaks, like the Gruenwald and so many other promontories mother spoke of and dreamed of with the knowledge she would never see those snowy crags again. Never would she visit six sisters, an aging father and the dear mother she loved. It must have been a constant weight on her heart.

Father, too, cherished the Swiss mountains. Somehow, I felt a driving kinship with alpine groves, poring over those calendars from Switzerland, there in the lamplight at Declo. The calendars came to us nearly every year in brown wrappers with stamps affixed. The stamps read "Helvetia." They seemed so different than ours, coming from a magic land I may never see.

What did mother's lullaby convey? Well, it said: "My little rabbit, why do you feel sorrowful—are you sad? You no longer jump, nor do you run (presumably with joy) in my garden. The rest is a rhythm pattern we find in some of our own popular songs like, Poo-poo-pa-doo!

The Good Samaritan who charged so little for her services visited the lonely shack until the patients were mended, as you'd say of a tinker's pot.

Neither of them ever forgot my mother. Maurine told her only boy what happened in that cabin among the rocks many times, I'm sure of that.

Years later, someone knocked at Dr. Droz's door. I was no longer around, having moved to Washington State. The caller was the grown version of mother's tiny patient of dry land days, a lieutenant colonel now, a graduate of West Point. "My mother and I spoke of you so many times," he said while he squeezed her hand. "Thank you for saving my life."

Chapter IV

The Bachelor Goes Home

What happened to Johann? I'm sure you want to know. The developments surprise me. He could have found another mate; I doubt he ever tried.

He stayed, as he'd promised, until the newlyweds strengthened their wings and jettisoned Cotterel forever.

This I believe: he no longer cared for pioneering in the American West, and neither do I. It's better to live where forests grow, where it *can* rain (and does frequently), in Puget Sound with the grand Olympics to gaze at. Saying all that, sometimes I miss the desert. I like to go back and ponder Cotterel.

The man whose dreams never came true left the desert forever. One day a tall, serious looking traveler boarded the train at Burley, bound for Alsace-Lorraine.

I must have seen him, wide eyed, as a baby sees, but never really knew him. None of us ever forgot him—a continual presence in my mind. I'm sure he saw me; that makes a difference too, a strange friendship of the most unusual kind; I feel close to a man I cannot consciously recall at all, who shared my trails on a brushy homestead.

I can imagine how Johann felt, taking one last glimpse, viewing weathered hills where the Point in turn stares stonily down on a dismal, decimated plateau with its two abandoned elevator stacks simmering in the sun.

I can vaguely imagine that man boarding the train at Burley, waving good-bye to one brother and a lost bride.

The locomotive leaves in a tantrum of clanging bells, spurting steam and staccato blasts, the way a grouse drums for attention. The lonely passenger watches meaningless ties slither and melt together, like taffy. He may pull a curtain for invading suns, but cannot shut Cotterel from his mind. Poe told the raven to take that beak from out of his heart; the raven croaked: "Nevermore!"

There is a haunting song, a recurring theme, linking my day-dreams of departed times. It's remarkable that I remember a tune, popular in World War I, when I was still in rompers.

My sisters played it on our portable phonograph, emanating from a huge horn poised above us. I'm indebted to a Poulsbo Librarian for locating this item in *Songs Of The Gilded Age*, edited by Margaret Bradford Boni and Norman Lloyd. The title is "Blue Bell" (words by Edward Madden, music by Theodore F. Morse). Caption reads: "Morse, a native of Washington D.C., ran away from Maryland Military Academy at the age of fourteen and went to New York. At fifteen his first composition was published, and by the time he was twenty-four he had become successful enough to have his own publishing business. 'Blue Bell' was the great Madden-Morse hit of the year 1904."

It was still a hit when we lived at Cotterel some ten years later, spurred on by a world war no military academy "action" could match. Here is that touching chorus:

> Good-bye, my Blue Bell. Farewell to you;
> One last look into your eyes so blue.
> 'Mid campfires gleaming, mid shot and shell,
> I will be dreaming of you, my Blue Bell.

As a child, I supposed "blue bells" referred to the flowers, but it paged a lady, not a plant. Nevertheless, the flower's effect and vague perfume remains in my mind when I hear it, a farewell to years and people of a far off time.

Those Edison-engendered notes wind onward like drifting smoke, under haunting stars, on a breeze scented with sage. All those paths that crossed mine have veered away, desert trails to nowhere; sand buries their track.

In the end, Johann said good-bye to the West and the girl who shared those dusty paths at Cotterel—a man who returned good for ill, who wanted a nest, a fire to dream by and golden-haired children. I fancy he shed a tear or two before returning to Alsace-Lorraine. There, my sisters say, he became a Lutheran minister.

<u>Author's note</u>: I did not create this story. It took hold of my thoughts and wrote its own conclusion, in a way. I remember that lovely girl and her husband. I visited them when my sisters were living with "M" for a brief time in Burley. Maurine's accent was quaint, marvelous and French, a ray of sunshine to everyone. I kept in touch with the family now and then as years spun by. She eventually had one daughter, beautiful as that girl at the depot. Unfortunately the daughter is gone. It's possible everyone of them is erased from the chalkboard of time, even as I write.

I played with that son, slightly younger than I, a handsome, mischievous lad who could tally up three or four lickings on one rainy day. You know how those days are; you sit and count raindrops with nothing left to do. A licking didn't seem to bother him as much as they worried me. He'd cry a few go rounds and head right back in mischief. He stayed at our house once; mother came into the bedroom to check us out. There he was, marching gleefully, with a kerosene lamp raised up over his head, romping about, apt to pitch the flaming lamp on our bed. Mother had a cat fit! He wasn't perturbed; for that matter, I wasn't either. But, as he grew, it was evident this chap had Horatio Alger genes, and grew handsomer with the years. He was nominated to attend West Point by Senator Borah, I think—but don't write that down. There are too many years getting in the way. I haven't seen that, mischievous fellow for a long time, but I'm sure we'd enjoy the memories. I think he had a tragic romance in his youth. There was a beautiful girl who was injured in a car crash and not his fault, but that is best left alone.

All those paths that once crossed mine have veered away like desert trails to nowhere, and sand buries the tracks. But I tell this story, before that happens, as a tribute to two people:

A man who loved and lost, who bore no grudge and returned good for ill.

AND

Mother, who told me much of this tale of Cotterel days. She was a Bible scholar, poet and doctor who ministered to many; a beacon in my life, who lived to the age of 107 and 1/2 years, plus 25 days. May she rest in peace.

THE SPELLCASTERS
or
Rain Follows The Plow

    Mother lit the cook stove when dogs began barking. She went to the window. A dust trail was creeping toward our homestead, "There's a wagon coming, Mama," Luke sang out from the vantage of a brush pile. My sisters remember just how the Gypsies came that day studying each dwelling as they passed, never camping too near, planning their visit to utilize every element of surprise. Thanks to another brother, we knew something about them before they arrived. Roy was hunting at the Pothole when four wagons rolled up the lane.
    A woman in bright clothing stepped to the screen. Her long, black hair sported two comely braids. She knocked, but nothing happened. The Gypsy yanked the latch; it held firm. She spied a child peering around a clothes rack.
    "Whe-a-r-r is yore mom-ma?" the voice was strange and harsh.
    "Mother went to the new house to see daddy!" May called with some trepidation.
    "Well den' lem-me in!" The visitor, sniffing the fumes of fresh baked bread, tugged harder on that pesky catch; it held again.
    May stepped in full view. "Mama said I mustn't let anyone come in!" She was small but chubby; resolute as the oldest girl has to be. She was minding mama, and that's mighty important when you're just seven years old—besides, she had a smaller sister and an infant brother in a crib to tend. Hadn't mother told her Gypsies were not to be trusted? Sometimes they kidnapped tiny babies—that was the story Europeans told.

The Gypsy rapped the door frame with both fists. Not a peep came from the children, retreating to a far corner. She tried a new tack. "I hav' a li'l-one—a sick one! Ple-e-z let me in!"

There was a painful pause. "I need bread for th' ba-bee? Yur mom-ma wooden' min'!" The caller knew if that girl opened the door a crack, she'd worm in; but May held firm as the lava beds beneath.

"No! I won't open the door!" She stamped a bare foot. The frustrated visitor rattled on the latch, made an ugly face and stuck out her tongue. May never expected to glimpse such a grand display; it was wrinkly, and orange-brown, like a cow's scooper-upper. How could anyone get that back in one jaw—without a crowbar?

The dark-skinned lady was grumpy; this child was impossible. She flounced off, strewing curses in the wind (who doesn't care how mortals fare) headed for a house in process of birthing. She heard the rap of dad's hammer.

This family was alert. Luke, sat on a wagon spring-seat with a twenty-two in tow. She simply ignored small fry.

Mother and the Gypsy finally connected. That prowler decided mother was no easier to deal with than her daughter. Olga Louise "D." got down to essentials in a whippa-jiffy.

"Do you really a have a sick baby?" mother queried. "If it's true, I'll examine your tot." May mentioned it was often a ruse Gypsies use to stir sympathy.

In spite of evident deception, mother invited the nomad into our tent; May watched with wonder filled eyes. Mother, smiling benignly, urged her guest to have a seat; brought her ward a bread loaf, one pound of rich butter and some knobby potatoes. We had little to give; the Gypsy was disappointed, no doubt.

The practitioner, trained from Romany's vales, felt she should act urbane though our gifts were mundane. Mother didn't bite when that city-wise schemer offered to blow good luck in mama's purse—a favorite routine. Soon the Gypsy, realizing little else would be forthcoming, offered a dimmed-down prophecy. In retrospect it went about so:

> "May good fortune ever reign
> In this hamlet on the plain."

Mother had a bias against charms and spells usually done for a fortune teller's fee. Her response was:

"It is nice you wish us well; however, I place my faith in God, our protector. I gain my "good luck," as you call it, by serving others in need whenever I can." It was true.

Suffice it to say, the spell that Gypsy levered, on our roof and our lands, was a bust. As plodding poets say so well:

> "Things were going great, I'm bound;
> Then, the weather turned around!"

We repeat, mother held poor opinion of wishful charms and omens, accompanied by fees. Here's a random thought. The Gypsy took no stock in talk of heavenly providence. Perhaps it was there all the time.[1]

---

[1] Perhaps longevity was a gift of providence. My mother is currently listed as the oldest Droz that ever lived in the entire world, courtesy of *Droz Family News*, Denver, Colorado: "Olga Droz, born Nov. 22-1870; died May 15-1978; 107 yr.; 6 Months; 25 days. (Information received, April 1975.)

Those were hard times in 1915. We had few amenities in this sage land home. Every gallon of water was a luxury, hauled by teams from Mark's well, quaffed with gusto while red suns sizzled on the rim-rock.

Here we approach an important secret. No one knew this for dozens of years; geologists never guessed it either when Mr. Rodenbaugh brought charts depicting The Cotterel Thrust Fault, in year 1931, at Southern Branch University in Pocatello, Idaho.

Directly under our burning shoe soles—three hundred feet down—nestled a phantom, a lake big enough to irrigate hundreds of acres. Above it, while we suffered, wry winds patrolled and tumbleweeds rolled.

Mr. Rodenbaugh never knew of that water source; being facetious for a moment:

> Some dowsers itch for a willow switch;
> I know that gambit well;
> Give one gypsy a slip and pour her a nip;
> And may that blithe spirit re-tell
> Where deep veins hie and cold springs 'ally'
> AND...
> Behold—a Bohemian spell!

No wonder the topsoil was dry; rainfall and snow melt immediately sank through porous sand, found a comfortable couch and sloshed fore and aft, seasons on end. Crops wilted; we sang songs of hope—prayed for rain. Even the un-churched joined in unison. As a child, I remember reciting this jingle—apropos the weather:

> Lord! Don't send us some plain clod-slosher;
> No! Lord, please grant us a 'Gully Washer'!

Father tossed all night after the Gypsy invasion. They really had a fling, dining on our food and handouts. Added to that, fortune tellers have a knack for garnering coins.

Finally, there in the fragrant sage of a Gypsy camp, (Zane Grey[1] dubbed it purple sage) the hubbub declined; the singing quelled. Fires flared, red embers sputtered out and sleep crept into each wanderer's nest. Twinkling stars and coyote serenades stood watch where the great dipper hung like a kitchen vessel in the milky way, empty as usual.

Looking back, one more time, I still admire those visitors whose roots lie in India. A book entitled Gypsies, Wanderers of the World by Bart McDowell, photographs by Bruce Dale, published by National Geographic Society, Washington D. C., has a foreword composed by an English Gypsy, Clifford Lee. It's a precious work defining the roles nomads played across the broad stage of the old world and our own times.

They were called quicksilver people—musicians and bear trainers, gold settlers, thieves, secretaries and engineers.

There were legions of poor Gypsies; some were untouchable in Indian climes. In European countries, trough makers hollowed out logs to feed-the-hogs, for one example. This was a rudimentary task. There were potters and pot menders; the list goes on and on.

By no means were all careers menial. Some Gypsies were financiers. One of the contributors to much of this tale was a scissors grinder who also kenned precious gems. Gypsies had rules of the road and taboos. It was not considered proper to rob a member of your group; still, it happened; on occasion

---

[1] Zane Grey (1875-1939), American novelist born in Zanesville, Ohio. He wrote about 60 books with a Western setting. One I remember best is Wanderer of the Wasteland.

someone broke that law and a gold ring eventually turned green.

Horse trading was much the same as in other lands. Let the buyer be aware, or beware! One unfortunate Gypsy traded for a horse who came down with "the heaves" in bad, wet weather. Horses get this from eating moldy feed. The sagacious trader, who sold only in dry weather, got it (the 'heavish' horse) back for a trifle in a wet winter and repeated the process, ad infinitum, from corral-to-corral.

<blockquote>So round and round she goes;
And toss in a few Ho! Ho's!</blockquote>

The best is this one. A schemer who passed a farmer's barnyard spied a very fine shoat. Says he, "Aha, there's a beauty; right for pit roast." From his coat pocket, wrapped in newspapers, he draws a fairly large sponge, dipped in lard, not swollen. He tosses it to the pig when no one's about. Pigs love lard; down goes the sponge for lard is slick.

The felon keeps an eye on that pig. In a short time, the pig falls ill. Finally the Gypsy comes up to the farmer and says.

"Seems to me the pig is sickly."

"Yes," says the owner, "He's come down with somethin' I never seen before."

The pig's stomach is swollen. He certainly is in pain. The Gypsy comes back and the hog is breathing it's last puffs. That sponge soaked up a lot of water. Fever from bound up insides made the hog drink more than ever. The sponge has swelled a great deal by now.

"Well, too bad!" says that sympathetic Gypsy. "I kin take him off ya hands, and bury 'im."

Report is, the ploy worked many times in many climes. Those porkers look mighty good on a spit. Hunting them "a-la-sponge" is one way to go. The price is right. No bill at all.

Weaving fortunes, casting spells, dispensing luck, both ill and good, as they chose. Such crafty schemes seem unique and oblique compared to a settler's plodding life.

Gypsies left their stamp in the minds of four children and a babe. Each one of us shared recollections of that pilgrimage to the "Point" by the nomads. In the twenties and thirties they camped on a vacant plot by our garden patch two miles from Declo, Idaho. They were traveling in large cars by now (some were Pierce Arrow size). How could they afford them? I'll never know.

I have one neighbor, I respect, who thinks I am too critical of Gypsies, I fear. If she reads this account, it will upset her. Truth is, there were many outstanding people of that descent in history. It is unfair to criticize everyone in any race for the shenanigans of a few. Individuals should be judged on their own merit.

To dispel her claim that I am over blowing the lifestyles of the personages in this account, Clifford Lee, the scissors grinder supports and outdoes anything I could bring up. He told many tales of their cunning and aptitude to survive. National Geographic produced a classic study, Copyright 1970. Standard Book Number 87044-088-8.

Sometimes I declare, in a joking manner, the Gypsies put a curse on Cotterel. Truth was: Our homestead, was doomed from the first settler on. There was a current saying of that day, promoting dry land speculation, that ran thus:

"Rain follows the plow," a headline of some sort. It was never suitable or fitting as Horace Greely's famous saw. "Go West Young Man! Go West!"

* * *

Colonel Parkinson was enthusiastic about dry farming in Idaho drylands. Many financiers, and railroad tycoons loved a canard of the rain and the plow doing a two-step together. How droll!

The yellow brick road, a tin man and the tremulously-limpid lion, surmounted by the ghost of Judy Garland...are far more believable than this mirage of 'bringing rain by scourging the plain.'

> A desert will bloom;
> So list to my cant;
> Clear brush; make room;
> Summarily plant.
>
> 'Ti's a harvest rhyme
> With grain in the shock;
> The rain's on time
> With Nature's clock.
>
> So join the pact;
> Till desert lands now!
> They'll soon bloom. In fact:
> (this is the canard)
> "Rain follows the plow!"

Repeat that last line. Isn't it catchy and up-beat. Well, it didn't apply to Cotterel. Only by careful planning and experience can a dry farmer succeed in that terrain. Deep well pumps cured the problem on Droz lands in after years, though we had lost our title by the time deep well pumps were used. A skilled dry land farmer treats his tract with all the considerations conductors grant Prima Donnas in areas where deep wells cannot function.

Three or four years after the first settler plowed our valley sod; dry fields succumbed to drought, tumbleweeds and desolation. Sam C's Cotterel City

Plat was never truly developed. The post office was disbanded. Exodus was pain.

The Gypsy visit of 1915, or thereabouts seemed orchestrated by Fate. In biblical times, a prophet came to alert the citizenry of events to be. If our Gypsies had only warned us; and if we'd then believed them. I like to fancy my family would have donned sackcloth and ashes and wept for mercy and guidance, on the day those wagons trailed across Cotterel casting spells and telling fortunes, that had no connection with our needs.

Ashes of their fires moldered away somewhere near our ranch. We arrived in 1914; by 1917 Cotterel was gutted. Yellow tumbleweeds began to reclaim the wilderness across miles of abandoned acreage Like those itinerant spell-casters, we did not wait for the final curtain; but struck our tents, and retreated, rambling like beggars cast out of Eden by bad weather. The exodus was done.

Though I was a babe between four and five years old this memory is clear. I remember songs the congregation sang at the last church services held in Cotterel; my choice was:

> Trying to walk in the steps of the Savior;
> Striving to follow my Savior and King.

Chorus was:

> How beau-ti-ful to walk
> In the steps of the Sa-viour,
> Step-ping in the light,
> Step-ping in the light...

The ending phrase was:

> ...Led in paths of light.

It sounded just right!

This song was by Eliza E. Hewett, 1851-1920 and Wm. J. Kirkpatrick, 1838-1921. Pump organs were inspiring; reeds had a brassy sound. A good resonance for Puritan voices. Only ancient coyote choirs ring across those hills today in rough-rocked enclaves. Still, my heart's there where sage boughs harbor the dove, and a prim cottontail rouses at dawn. I cannot go on. This all sounds out-of-tune eight-tenths of a lifetime later.

Leave my memories there;
The Gypsies won't care.

SONS OF THE LAND
I. The Point

Afternoon light poured down the draw and sunbursts of mica glinted across a ledge in outcrops near the rim-rock. A feather fluttered down, teetered on a juniper limb and tumbled to oblivion. A locoweed rattled from impacts of a red-winged grasshopper. Cicadas trilled in rocks speckled with lichen. Jim Hill mustards bobbed mysteriously, signs of a scuttling lizard. The magpie, sans one tail feather, flew to a stump where some settler had cut down a stately tree. There, it performed a mocking tirade; jeering at blue skies and puff-white clouds, draining all the mischief it could muster. His mate jibbered from a dry limb where a sphinx moth, with blue half-moons incised on two of its wings, uncoiled its proboscis and sipped a lupine blossom. Unlike most moths, who favor nights on the town, they sup in broad daylight. The lad decided they were vain-and-urbane, unduly proud of those iridescent colors.

The red mare was breathing hard. Here was the summit. How pleasant to feel the canyon breeze, relaxing in the shade of an incense spreading juniper. The boy slid off the sweating mare, whistling the Ol' Chisholm Trail chorus of "Cum a ti, yi yip!" It had been a steep ride up the mountain grade east of Dewey's ranch.

He'd been a'horse three hours. Those patched and holey overalls were wet; he was galled with the heat-and-acid of a nag's sweaty hide. Almost all the lads I knew rode bare back all summer long. That's why we loved swimmin' to cool our ulteriors. He sprawled on dry juniper needles, loving the view; talking to that mare who bobbed her head every now and again. She wasn't really answering, just shaking off pesky gnats, which drive farm animals bananas in summer. "That's bad, Maudie," the lad opined. "I'll grease your chin and mustache when we get home."

Mares have their own private thoughts and pursuits unknown to me. It was plain she loved the mountain. As for the boy whose weight she bore without complaint, I had designs of my own, thinking to be an entomologist. I doubt a true butterfly connoisseur ever set foot on Cotterel Mountain before or since. Here was a farm boy who should have been hoeing beets, idly searching for butterflies with a home-made cheese cloth net.

Many boys caught them in their caps for deviltry and mayhem. The prize sought was a white flier with green veined wings. They were hard to find even then.

A yellow striped *papilio rutulus* swallowtail drifted over; but he never tempted the netteree. He watched this zebra striped flower bandit glide from view. "It's probably stuffed to the hubs with sugar from Dewey's lilacs," the lad told the mare. Maude just shook her head to rout the gnats, a convenient finale, proving she agreed.

They were near the "Point" at Cotterel, visible for miles. He gazed on patchworks to the west. Then cast his eyes eastward, spotting Heglar hills, in the distance, and nearby potholes on the Humbert-Droz tract. It was a panorama of batholiths, scattered, rocky patches of untended sage and ploughed fields. Some were green oases; others were brown clods, waiting out idle years, before another planting spree.

Dry farmers have a knack for raising grain in that area. When we came there, fresh from city ways, we stood little chance of coping with wet and dry seasons, winds that uncover sprouting seed and a host of bedevilments too boring to mention.

That lad on the mountain let his mind drift to the earlier time when we endured the dry spell of about 1915, on the homestead we lost.

Over the lip of that mountain's, north-most jut, lay a rail road cut engineered by gandy dancers and railroad entrepreneurs around 1909. The deep trench involved men, horses, locomotives, dynamite and belching steam cranes. The rails were knitted to ties on a very sharp curve. A siding was planned for Cotterel and a grain elevator was built with great expectations in tow.

Seeing no reason to linger long in this lonely spot, however, the rails departed for Idahome. That was truly a mistake. You could fry eggs on those steel bars in summer. The sun had a nip; there was a batch of vacant, useless land, cowboys named Cactus Flat, a wide and lonely expanse on the way to Malta. A cowboy with his foot caught in a stirrup, was dragged to death and buried in this dismal locale. A wagon tie rod, driven deep, marked his mound for a decade. He was too full of spines for an undertaker, perhaps a rambling cowpoke short of money.

Truth was this "railroad boom" was bound to bust. And it did! For a quarter century that terrain was mainly cattle graze land in spring where purple June grass waved windy good-byes to the traveler in a Lizzie headed for city life and the irrigated valleys of Utah.

So the single-tracks-fiasco halted at Idahome and gave up the ghost at the grain elevator near line's end. I once slept in there, a derelict shell, after interior partitions were dismantled, working a few days for a chap who later became a partner with my brother on a cattle enterprise. His name was Frank Coffey, a somewhat jovial and most enterprising Burley auctioneer, connoisseur of mules, horses and cattle.

Frank had contracted to hire teamsters feeding a

noisy rock crusher in a pit carved in low sage at Idahome. My brother, Luke, had signed up to run four head of mules on a Fresno, a most ungainly, stubborn and man-killing device. Luke sent me instead. There hangs another unfinished tale. I will never forget the heat, turmoil and grim-grind of going round-and-round in a rocky pit. There is dust, racket and danger; an occasional snake slithers past. You step over a pipe-grate hopper, balancing your scraper at the lip of this act, urging those weary mules with reins in one fist, with your right hand welded on a weasely "Johnson" bar (Fresno handle-lever). Your throat's powder dry. It's around 105, or so it looks; and the evening horn—will it ever sound?

I've really digressed; we'll return to the boy on the mount in a moment. Suffice it to say Frank Coffey knew that job was too heavy for one farm boy weighing only one-hundred and thirty-five pounds saddled with a gimpy hip. He fed the crew of teamsters, and housed some of us for free in the vacated ruins of Idahome's only grain elevator. I had my packet there. About the end of the third day, I knew I was done in. Frank came over the following morning and said, "Well, Dwight, I'm heading for Burley this morning. Would you like to take a ride home with me? Better bring your pack."

I was never fired. We talked about a lot of things of small consequence. One last statement he made was; "I never had a man who tried harder than you did!" It was probably true; Luke should have been strung by the thumbs for a fortnight. He never even batted an eye when I came home. Boogering a team hooked on that cantankerous earth mover-scraper, with a steel lever threshing about, is a weak substitute for a pleasant stroll through Disneyland! Please believe it; hanging on the reins to four wise mules, urging them, balancing your Fresno full of "up-and-down" shenanigans, is a very tricky feat; you really need an extra pair of mitts for these skits; please leave it there.

The lad looked beyond nearby hills, scanning the arc of Heglar Mountains. Somewhere down in one brushy goolagong, a graveled highway struggled southward toward Strevell. Once, perhaps, railway engineers hoped that band of ties, rippling in heat waves would eventually continue clear to the border of Utah; instead, they trickled away into mental mists of "No-land." That ambling road was the sole route to Ogden and Salt Lake City. There's a load of lonesome country in Southern Idaho. Foothills are full of tempting valleys, a grand spot to abort the roaring crowd.

A steam crane, lifting chunks of stone in multiple tons, did Cotterel historians a favor. Though the project destroyed most of the Indian\Pioneer trail, a few original ruts remain. Some of the rocks it removed were so huge, they remained a crane-reach from the track, right in the center of that original trail. Settlers ploughed adjacent land, but these huge rocks posed too much work. Because of this, a narrow strip of the combined Indian Trace is still visible, just below the Point. I re-checked the site in 1980, revisiting Cotterel the same day. You must enter private land to arrive where two cement stacks bristle, like the towers of a crumbling castle.

I often ponder on the danger desert fauna and flora face everywhere. The horned toad is threatened. Does that white butterfly with veins of green in each wing still fly among the lupine? Once there were many varieties of white butterflies crisscrossing America, When *pieris rapae*, a pest of the cabbage world with two black dots anchored in the upper wings, was accidentally imported from Europe, without tickets or baggage, butterfly society turned end over end. One white butterfly species, that flew in large numbers, nearly, disappeared....

That cabbage-eater crosses and re-crosses every American garden, universally common. That is a byte of what the lad thought, gazing down on a troubled valley. Then, he remembered tales of the settlers (circa 1915) who, like that impromptu butterfly, seemed to melt in the mist.

Mountain top reveries of historians and dreamers, sitting under a juniper at Cotterel Point, are sometimes traumatic. Other times they inspire us. Beloved forms and faces come to mind, mingle with clouds and shadows and disappear.

That lad in overalls, fully rested, climbs back on the spine of that sure footed mare, picking her way through those scented glades. Rim-rock sleeps eternally and boredom binds the hill. Civilization closes in once more.

II. Santa Clause Adams, The Hermit

There once was a hermit—a true one—who lived in a grove where Marshcreek crosses the fences of Dewey Ranch.

The property was tremendous. It occupied 1,750 acres formerly owned by a widow, Mrs. S. R. Gwinn. At the time an Astorian explorer, named Stuart, first crossed here in 1828, it teemed with wildlife. Mountain lion, deer, beaver and various species of wildfowl, including the near extinct blue heron, once filled this valley west of Cotterel mountain. Mr. Dewey took possession on January 1, 1909 and increased the spread to more than 20,000 acres by homestead, land purchase and leasing. They held sway there for 65 years.

I mentioned that boy and his lively mare climbing the mountain over Dewey's, remembering the ghosts of settlers departed. Well, there is a hermetic ghost with the most flowing white beard of all the kingdoms whose restless spirit still haunts these hills. I wot. This indomitable live-aloner settled by a hot spring just inside the southern edge of Dewey land, as I remember it. His last name was Adams. I don't believe any one lists his first name. Declo folks called him "Santa Claus" Adams, honoring that unique, tres-chic beard.

Dad drove the Humbert-Droz clan up to Dewey's in a vintage Maxwell that comedian, Jack Benny, twitted by radio a few years hence. That Fourth of July was a memorable day.

Mother and dad, two sisters and two brothers, plus yours truly, held our patriotic, celebration where the rippling waters of Marsh creek course through tree-lined groves (there at Dewey's). I didn't know all but three of us would disappear in just a few million ticks of Father Time.

The creek ran ankle high in wide places; waist high in the narrow necks. Droz children splash and wade across bands of twinkling pebbles. We built dams in the riffles where crawdads exited, with pincers waving good-bye. Some were bucketed, we released them in the end.

The hermit's fence ran nearby; braying genets (also called jennets) lumbered up, hoping for handouts. Old Adams must have raised them by habit. I don't know what use they were at this stage of his life. He was very old; the roaming years were done. Local historians say most of his goings and comings reflect only mystery. Where did he hail from; people place much importance on traits and dates? Mr. Adams didn't dwell on his life history. Perhaps Missouri drove his tap roots in that deep sod; Ed Vallette met him there on a riverboat in the 1880's. Old hirsute Adams kept a pack of curs for his protection. Exactly put: "Adams kept a pack of cur dogs for no apparent reason—for company perhaps. There were from ten to fifteen dogs all the time, and sometimes, as many as 30 or 40. Some of them were vicious to strangers" (*Declo, My Town, My People,* "Biographies," page 139).

I concur completely. They weren't lovable; let me tell you. They were a growlish, glowering batch of assassins, primed to devour werewolves when the moon was right.

One sister-in-law, in Idaho, escorted me to Nampa Library for historical follow up. There, I came across a book written, of all things, by a chap from Albion, Idaho, a very blithe spirit was he.

The author was Bill Bailey. In the history of his valley (Albion), he spoke of a chap named Jiggs, a very big and pleasant fellow, I remember, who once ran a service station in that vale. A few mots later, he mentioned Homer Haller. What a surprise. I boarded with Homer one winter while attending Albion Normal School.

Bill's rollicking book entitled *Bill Bailey Came Home* (Publisher unknown; check Nampa Library) is brimful of Cassia County lore; I enjoyed everything penned, including a sketch map of Albion valley dated 1905. There lay Dewey Ranch, including an X to mark the precise spot where Hermit Adams settled many years ago. That terrain was close to our Droz family homestead, a short crow-flight over narrow Cotterel Mountain.

There on that home-cured map lay Howell's creek. I mention the creek in The Hymn of Harrison Valley.

Follow Howell's creek on that map as you head for Albion town. Cross to Marshcreek; saunter northward. Presto, you're at Dewey's where the hermit waits.

Guess what? Bill Bailey, a trapper-boy at fifteen, told how he once trekked that course to Deweys; trapping muskrat and other beasties was on his mind for that trip. His small pooch was in tow; he had a bundle of traps in a shoulder sack, the last part is my guess. Suddenly, this wolflike pack, the Adams tribe, rushed up-gulch to greet innocent William; friendly pats were no motive. Those poodlers planned to meat (a bad pun verbus) him!

They intended to save the punious-pup for soup-and-dessert. The little dog cowered behind his shaking chum. Bill made this scary episode the heartbeat of one chapter. Everyone who ever saw that pack seems anxious to rehash the episode, so do I.

Adams was no Rasputin! He was a threat to no one. There was an unusual aroma and flair about him that you do not spot in the local lot of a shopping mart. Bill was shocked when a pack of hyenaic-mongrels, burst from the blue and penned him in a grove. It appeared that:

> He was about to meet his Maker;
> Don't negate the undertaker!

Right then, Old Man Adams, with that shaggy beard, flowering to his waist, hove in view, clutching a baton. His wild, hermetic whoops made the canyon ring.

Bill Bailey, like every other party threatened by those mutts, was badly frightened.

As Bill tells it, the old man rapped some noses. Then he pointed a stern finger at the leader, a cur with slitted eyes. He barks out the name of the beast. The burly brute shudders, folds his fangs and slinks away. The band falters now with lowered head, and tail a'droop. Every time the story reappears, someone adds a dog. No hermitage beast ever devoured an entire tourist, but some tried a nippet. That's my surmise.

Bill Bailey and "Socratic" Adams (who knew exactly when to open his mouth—and the best time to keep it shut), had a good talk that day.

As usual, he skirted questions about family ties, but easily swapped news with the local guys. Now, let's return to a Fourth of July picnic with Drozes in tow.

Descendants of the Adams clan of guardian dogs rushed out to celebrate our arrival. The hermit arrived on-cue, toting a walking stick, doing double duty as a club. If you were bored with calm life on the flats below, this eruption of barks and snarls formed a good excuse to fetch your gal, visit the hermitage and sniff the juniper-berry air, a unique scent of Christmas trees cut yearly.

Mysterious Mr. "A" was tallish still. Weathered like a fire-charred cedar shard, you couldn't guess his age, hidden in the thatchment of a very-bleary-beard. So, few clews appeared. The Levis were traditional, but he had no shirt, I ween. I didn't say he was naked. On that hot July afternoon our subject was amply protected by a fixture J. C. Penney sold all over America, in the "plenty-twenties," (early part) called B.V.D.'s with the button flap seat.

Mother ignored his clothes. She'd seen unusual behavior on two continents, and figured the old man was a harmless recluse.

He remained a mystery. That was his charm. Was he robber—thief; or Zennish zealot? No one could solve the riddle.

I was there when he talked of mountain men and Indians; he told of buffaloes sunning in wallows along the Snake. I think he mentioned buffalo tea. When those behemoths march ahead of your stream, in a day-long parade, the water grows "tea-like" and turns a bit green. I'll say no more of that topic!

Old Adams told us one of the Greener boys of Declo camped at his place for a week that season; he did entertain guests on occasion. The shack, some named it that, looked like a dugout to me. It may have evolved, a mite, as years wore on. Deweys were friendly and brought him supplies.

"Do you get away often?" mother queried.

He shook that shaggy head. "I haven't been to Declo for twenty years." The dugout was a grim place where he rusted as years toppled by, piling like snow, unseen in the night. His beard grew longer and more concealing.

Mother asked if he enjoyed bathing in the hot spring sluicing past his door.

"I'm afraid that would shock my heart," he replied. He was soft-spoken and well-mannered. His speech was effective and informative.

Mother was well impressed. He was the last of the pioneers before my parent's time. Santa Claus Adams died sometime after 1917, say some historians. I believe he lived beyond that date. He died unknown—mired in a den of quarrelsome dogs; blessed by the friendly company of mercifully placid jennets (a female burrow) and jacks. Old Santa Claus indeed! He was a long way short of Christmas; that obscure, lonely soul—an icon of frontier-oddity on the Covered Wagon Trail.

III. Trapper and Rancher

On that mountain above Cotterel another Droz was wont to ride. He was seventeen or so on the day we meet him here, well-muscled and over six feet tall. A western sombrero made him seem taller. He wore high-top boots for walking, not riding, and a sheepskin lined mackinaw. It was November; harvest was over; time to run trap line, for furs were in prime.

He climbed down from the sorrel gelding and untied the saddle strings. Then he lowered a gunny sack to the ground and tethered his mount to a juniper bough. Roy Droz, oldest son of Robert Humbert-Droz, a homesteader, helped clear off the brush and rocks at Cotterel. Settler's sons, starting as early as age nine, soon learned to drive a gentled team usually hitched to a stone boat (horse drawn sled).

Unlike a few weird aberrations in families, Roy paid scant attention to butterflies; his eyes leaped at the sight of a thirty-thirty rifle. His love was the hunt, the chase, the capture and the calm when a furry animal lay comatose, and its skin was strapped on a drying frame, or mayhaps, tacked on a wall like a flat badger hide; now that was beautiful, meaningful and money prone. Those things are all linked together as you will see. That is the formula on which you build a tycoon and that's what Roy became.

Perhaps this is a bit of a roast. I underwent a few trying years under the wings of two older brothers. Both are gone now, and God bless them; that's my hope. Roy liked music. He was no bumpkin which I seemed to infer. Not at all:

> Product of poor times, slow-won,
> Roy always helped! The oldest son.
> He didn't stand on shifting sand;
> The bugger wouldn't run!
> He had the eye old eagles vie—
> A crack-shot with a gun!
> As a lad, he worked all day
> On a Cotterel homestead sans no pay.
> That is how he helped our dad
> Build a home. A dream we had!

Thanks for your pains. A job well done!
That is the way our West was won!

By now, you must know Roy was a trapper of great skill. We now change tense: Beside the pungent scent of sagy wood fires, what is that curious smell permeating his boots, dungarees and hunting paraphernalia? Along with two sacks of coyote traps, used in winter forays, he carried a small, tightly-capped bottle filled frequently from a huge can of minnows left to rot in a corner by the hog shed. It melded with wood smoke, liniment and horse sweat. You never find smells like these in the city salon or a pub. I mentioned rotten minnows but coyotes have class. To lure them a trifle, his recipe called for four ounces of asafetida, some oil of sweet anise and sundry items—equally potent—a powerful, cloying souciant I will never forget.

An old trapper passed this secret to Roy on some long, winter evening. Perhaps it dates back to frolicsome mountain men, who can say? Roy had a touch of father's charm when needed. He also had a strong forearm if the need arose. He made friends more than enemies, a good rule of thumb. He was an excellent horse trader, not over sentimental, a man of strong principle.

There was a lot of trap line to run and a long ride home again. He also liked the red mare to carry him with a pack tied on the saddle. His artistry was to set a trap with precision and skill, stepping carefully to avoid leaving footprints in the trail and cloaking man-smells with wood fires and bait. His hat and gloves were smoked with sage and juniper wood before he debarked.

Watch him scoop a shallow trench in the earth, scattering fragrant needles as he works. From a tote sack he removes a double-spring trap attached to three feet of chain. The artisan places the trap over his right knee. Gripping the springs, firmly, one in each strong fist, he squeezes until the jaws flutter open. This is a Victor trap with a large V punched in the center pad. If a trap is extremely stiff, he uses his feet to depress the springs. When the trap is opened (before it is fully locked), it is difficult to keep both springs depressed. Where does he get a free hand? The trap is on the ground now. He must shove one foot over a spring; presto, the left or right hand is free. There is a two-and-a-half-inch narrow bar coupled to the bottom of that mechanism of capture. He must engage the flat end of that bar in a notch. The notch is machined into a pad device where the bait is offered. When engaged properly, the trap is tensed and ready to fire. If the bar does not lock properly, if the metal pad drops down, the trap springs shut on the trappers "paws", not a good practice.

So the trap is cocked and waiting for prey. He settles it evenly and carefully in the trench. He must be sure it is obscured, not buried, but lightly covered. He places a layer of smoked newsprint from the Sears Catalog, summer edition—perhaps the lingerie division is thinner paper. He carefully covers the jaws and springs with a tasteful sifting of earth. Too much weight will depress the bait pad and fire the trap.

Last, he scatters a few sticks, chaff and earth over the doctored area so it appears untouched as before. He brushes the entire vicinity with a leafed branch to obliterate tracks and level depressions.

What an artist the old time trapper was. There was much more to the trapper's bag of lore. He must reconstruct in his mind how a certain animal will approach, where it may stop to sniff, where it would urinate to leave a sign, and even guess at places it would naturally leap over an obstacle in the trail.

Now he must decide where it would land. That would be a fine place for a trap. The most important procedure of all is this one: he secures the catching device with a metal stake or chains it to a stump. More often, he attaches a three-pronged metal hook to the chain designed to catch in brush.

He is constantly reading sign, marks of a foot pad, bones where a kill was devoured, signs of a den. It is customary for a trapper to have fifty or more traps in a string of sets running along the rim-rock through juniper scrub and on down the canyon into sagebrush of a prairie that spreads over foothills for many miles.

Now comes the hard part, a daily trek down the lines to gather the game, repair sprung traps and rescue trapped animals from predators and themselves. If left long enough, they may gnaw themselves loose.

I am not justifying or glorifying a trapper's credo. To me it was and always will be repulsive, but the open air and adventure of riding wild boundaries was appealing. I always felt sorry for the animals but often rode with Roy; after all, he was my oldest brother. He bought one roadster after another when riding a horse on mountain runs began to pall. The lynx, commonly called a bobcat, were decimated by now.

At one time there were three of us, all, reasonably adjusted to life out of doors. Now, I alone remain. Dad's oldest son was a doer, a giant of determination, in my childish eyes, full of drive and

116

know-how. I was a scriber and dreamer.

Roy was no environmentalist; I doubt he could have changed. So long as the muskrat, lynx or coyote ran the canyon rim, or swam the streams, he was programmed to hunt them down. It was not a matter of malice. Hunting was entrenched deep in him as a way of life. A fast-moving truck in a smoke-filled intersection removed him from earthly endeavors. He will set trap no more. Those keen eyes will never drop a wild deer; his sun has set ever more.

IV. Wilderness

How swiftly the sun climbs the desert hill and launches into pink skies. From the moment the east lightens, and waking birds flutter from a branch, hubbub ensues. Wide-eyed sunflowers spill their scents on a morning glade. The gopher bustles from his mound and scurries up-ridge to nibble June-tender sprigs of grass. Out of rich earth, a badger plows a ridge with brown-red crumbs still riding on his nose. Those gleaming eyes, under shaggy brows, on a low forehead, mark him a dunderhead—which he is not. He's burrow-wise and feared by all. He conjectures all's right above his door, though he scarcely fears the coyote, and essays out with a trace of a swagger. All cogent rodents beat a noisy retreat.

He's an insatiable "tunneleer." Old Badger is a rodent-gourmet and pirate, too. If he's overlooked, and not over booked, his visit can cost your life and leave your wife a burrow-widow. Flat, long-clawed and hard-muscled, he seems uninspiring-and-untiring in his search for warm and furry fare.

After that first flush of pink, the sky brightens quickly and the warm rays pour down golden shafts, suffusing the tips of the butte as shadows flutter and steal away. The owl seeks his burrow, for a brief nap.

The mother coyote trots homeward to nuzzle and nurse her cubs after the night's carouse. Strange how each mother, no matter how fierce and unrelenting is her stalk, can turn the tables and lick those furry babes like an angel of mercy and light.

The cedars stand silhouetted in morning prayer, and a puff of cloud spreads its robe and kneels at the lip of the void where the last frail star of the morn flickers like a stricken candle and, too, steals away.

The mourning dove croons softly near the sage-scented nest, while a snaggle of weary-eyed male, coyotes, spent by their all-night vigil, set up their final orgy of yaps, defiant of day.

Never too near, always just beyond your eyes, comfortably out of reach, their mystic voices are the most primitive, lonely sounds I long to hear again, deep in a glen, where the wilderness whispers amen.

"These are my tracks," he muttered to no one. I'm lost!"

LOST IN A STORM

About the fall of 1928 my youngest sister, Dora, obtained a teaching position in an isolated settlement, predominantly Mormon. It was a higher elevation than Declo and the last place Dora desired. She liked bigger places and bright lights, but here she was. After rooming with parents of students for a while, she was able to obtain a batching cabin, allowing her independent spirit to assert its will.

We brought her supplies now and then with the Model 'T' Ford and Dora got settled into new quarters in spite of primitive accommodations. She cooked on a wood stove and her cabin was small; however, she put up new curtains and felt prepared for winter. No one realized what lay ahead.

An unusual cold front bottled up the entire Snake River Basin and snow soon blanketed the high country. A wild, west wind pummeled the poplars by our house, and snow drifts bogged the lanes so cars were of no use. It was one of those hard winters old timers talk about for years, bitterly cold and snow laden.

When mail came through, we finally received word that Dora was low on supplies up there in Malta, a very small place.

We discussed the problem at supper time. Mama was worried too. More storms were predicted; we knew snow was drifting, even as we talked, on the flats beyond Cotterel. Sister was snowbound, and so were we; and she was forty miles away.

"We've got to help," father said to my brother. "I know the Ford can't get through. What will we do?"

Luke, seven years older than I, was a sturdy fellow of stubborn and determined nature. He pondered a while, then said, "I'll leave tomorrow morning," and that was that.

Dad had to agree it was necessary, but no one realized how bad the storm would be and how deep the snow would get on Cactus Flats and that's where Luke was headed. He just went to bed like it was no big thing. He was not the type to worry.

Mother was relieved. She and father gathered jars of fruit and staples, home-baked bread and a host of things for Dora. Next day Luke set out early, early for him that is. He liked to lie abed on cold winter mornings, but dutifully loaded the wagon box on that bobsled frame with help from two of us. He forked in hay and bundled up for a cold ride. Hitching up a tough duo named Barney and Bill, he headed out with sleet plastering him white before he even reached the bridge beyond our lane.

One thing was in his favor—a tail wind. For that we were thankful. He knew the country like a babe knows the cradle and headed for the Point at Cotterel. We knew people at Idahome. He could always stay there if need arose. He was resourceful but he didn't foresee the unusual events to come that very day.

The sky was bleak enough. The wind did not abate. That valiant team trotted briskly at first. Six miles or so later Luke went around the Point and veered to the right. Now, the wind battered the sled from the side and drifts feathered diagonally across his path. The horses struggled on.

There, somewhere on the old highway to Ogden, he encountered a problem, not of his making—not in the plan—a stranded car and two men struggling to push it through the drifts.

Brother, bless him, was never one to shun a fellow in need. The driver's wife was seriously ill. The trio were headed for Burley hospital. Luke forgot his own urgent errand for the time and hooked his team to the stranded auto going back to where he'd been, with his horses facing the full blast of the storm.

I never learned how much time brother lost but every hour counted a lot that day. Fortunately, someone came by who volunteered to help those folks get through. Luke turned around and headed for Idahome in a hurry. He knew he'd lost time. Maybe he was careless because he hurried as we just mentioned. In any event, he veered off the road in the blind-whiteness. The snowflakes were close together now and vision was blurred. This was unfenced land with no visible boundaries. He couldn't tell exactly where the road was, but Luke figured he was on track or near to it. He wound on west of Heglar, he guessed, in a never-land of white. Then his heart leaped. He must be going right; here were fresh tracks!

He jumped off the sleigh to get his bearings; then it dawned on him.

"These are my tracks," he muttered to no one. "I'm lost!"

Where had the day gone? His hands and feet were growing numb; he stomped and swung his arms to warm up. The horses were tiring and felt the cold. He wondered if he should turn around and head for home.

Luke thought a while and rested the team. He decided to keep going as planned. He judged his compass direction by remembering how winds usually travel here; and, in the main, he was tracking right—but would he ever find a place to get out of the storm in time? That is the point of my story. Our lives, in such a bind, dangle on a sliver. Something unforeseen is needed to snatch us from oblivion—what will it be? Will we survive? It was growing dark. He'd lost valuable time playing Good Samaritan, to get those folks to Burley. He felt real panic.

When all seemed hopeless, and my sister

remembers this as I do, Luke said he saw something unbelievable—the near thing to a miracle for a guy who never believed in them. He spied something, a faint glimmer, way off in the dusk in all that driving snow and he knew he shouldn't see it. It was crazy to think he did; then he caught it again just when Luke decided he was a fool.

That was lonely country; could it be true—a marker? He peered into the dusk, the light was gone. He could barely see shadowy shapes of the team in that driving snow.

What's there to lose, he thought, heading toward the spot where the light had been? It was as good as any other choice. It seemed an eternity passed; then, the elusive light blinked again. He'd reached the home of the Abbot family—and not a fig too soon. He was about done in and so was the team. The storm had done its best, but there was no victim for this time.

Abbots came out, got the horses under cover, took Luke in the house with a lot of commotion, thawed him out, fed him and rolled out his bedroll. They were surprised he was traveling on a night like this.

He got up late next morning; the weather calmed. The horses were able to go, though stiff at the start. By this time, other teams had opened the road. Luke headed up Bull Lane in the afternoon. (As I remember it, the fences on that lane had an antique brand of wire called Scutt's Wooden Block. It really did have a thin, block of wood, grooved to fit between two twisted wires as if in a frame, and alternating with an arrowhead shaped four-point iron barb, stamped from flat sheet metal and twisted into that showy display collectors now love to frame on the wall—rare antiques today. That block was placed there so cattle would see it and veer away. Wooden blocks rotted and fell off after a decade or two. The only good ones left are in wire museums and private collections.)

Dora was certainly glad to see her brother and those supplies so badly needed. She never thought Luke would brave such a storm. I'll be very clear on this. My brother was extremely near-sighted. This marked trait was a curse all his life. My sister and I were surprised at what he told us of that night and the storm. He is gone, and we cannot check for details. He wasn't one to talk about miracles. That land was a big space to be lost in. We only know that light he saw, or thought he saw, when he was (maybe) too far away to see it, that light saved his life!

That was supposed to be the capper; the ending line when I composed this memoir many years ago. I phoned my sister a couple years back when I was revising the copy. As we reviewed what I'd narrated we got a laugh and a couple surprises. I suddenly remembered Luke told me he let the lines go lax as night fell, to let the horses drift a time; this was a vital point. Then, another fact surfaced, maybe Dora brought it up: My brother was worried about the horses when he arrived at Abbots. He moved his bedroll to a straw pile in the barn to keep watch on his team. The Abbots tried to dissuade him; as usual, he was stubborn.

It was very cold out there; he was foolish. Straw barns are drafty. But he survived every twist of Fate.

Luke wondered why it felt so warm. He woke toasty, and rested. Then came a blast of massive grunts and his bedroll erupted! A monstrous, squealing sow and one passel of piglets popped out of the straw and dove for the door. Can you top that pig-tale? After some thought, I doubted this was all happenstance. There's a moving pattern here, call it what you may.

Seems to me Luke had used all the luck in mystery's-lamp. Genie or none, my brother had won a very hard run by the time his spent team staggered up to a small ranch dome near a hamlet folks call Idahome. First, he saw a light glimmering far away. Then, to top it off, he traded a spicy nest in the Abbotian parlor for a bedroll in a cold shed—he was dead-beat, fagged out!

Seems to me someone like that Dame 'Good Deed' rewarded his endeavor of dragging jitneys through drifts to save a woman's life. Did that sway or stay her wand? In any case, the weary driver with a blue-stubbled chin tossed his bedroll on a straw pile as:

>Gory gouts of steam unroll
>From a Gaucho, very "sloucho"
>On a porky fumerole;
>How droll.

He was ignorant and happy. That's how we usually were, gallumping about in the Nineteen-Twenties. It was a time when country folks dreamed of angels. And why not? There still may be a few way back in the hills at Cotterel.

H.B. Scutt's Wooden Block (patented February 10, 1880); the barb adjacent to the block was a Scutt's Arrowplate Barb. Illustration from: *The Bobbed Wire Bible, VI*, by Jack Glover (April 1980, illustration #48).

SNAKE KILLER FROM CHEYENNE

She was a comely bay mare from Cheyenne, Wyoming, wearing a "wine-cup" brand. Some frontier blacksmith must have enjoyed forming that unusually-attractive metal ornament, a branding iron that smote her hip with smoky-hiss and left an inner mark of malaise in her psyche. That mare remained jumpy from that time on. She shied at every imaginable spook on trails my brothers rode.

Her peripheral vision was unique. When she pulled the buggy with old Tom, she seemed to see right through the cumbersome blinder pads attached to the bridles of every harness we owned; they were intended to shut off side vision, especially for spooky horses.

Shy, as you may have guessed, was clipped from the town named "Cheyenne," and fit her wily spirit perfectly. She could pull plows, drag harrows and even "stone-boats" for moving rock, but that nubile mare much preferred romping in the shalves of a buggy or doubling on the tongue of a two-seater with a tasseled top. This was lighter duty and she was in her glory, running happy as a bounding rabbit.

One day Roy set out with Tom and Shy from our house to the Schrenk homestead. Dad was dozing when they swung onto a cutoff full of weeds, trash and mayhem. Cheyenne, prancing on the right, suddenly snorted and struck like a thunderbolt with her left hind foot. Was it a shiny tin can, a piece of bright paper or a scrap of bottle glass? She was always "skid-dooing" from something—anything. Dad snapped awake and jumped off the buggy. There by his left boot lay a half-stunned rattler coilin'-and-cussin'. Pop dispatched him with a rock.

From that time on pa was proud of that mare, a dead-shot with a mean dislike for snakes.

"Rattle-toters" with lots of buttons were commonplace everywhere you drove in 1914-15. You never donned boot's, when you rose from your bedroll at dawn, without turning 'em over and shaking them like a cocktail. We always took a quick look-see for snakes when meandering through rock piles and brush. "Fangers" were anxious to avoid us, too; that's my contention, and I've encountered a few in my lifetime. Today, sighting a rattler is a rare event.

After I was injured, on the drylands, mother conveyed me to Boise via U.P. We rode in a baggage car for I could not walk. I was too heavy to carry—my injury hung on for years.

The trainmen were most considerate. Father remained home to look after Roy, Luke, May and Dora; to prepare meals daily and keep the peace. He was absent during weekdays. Carpenter wages kept our family solvent. The crops were failing.

When he returned one evening, our milk cow was gone. Father stayed home next morning; between mending fences and tidying the house he searched for that wayward drifter.

That evening, dad lit the lantern and searched the garden even the pothole that could swallow a train and crew.

There were only 320 acres of Droz land out there. Fact was, like that fabled "Wreck of the Hesperus," one critter, "poetically put," had "sunk beneath the wave." (I remember ol' "Hesperus." Luke memorized it in the seventh grade when we shared one bedroom.)

When dad trudged in, raised the globe and blew the lantern, his eyes were red; his lips were cracked from a nagging wind.

This was the first time my sister, Dora, ever saw

my Father cry. She re-lived that incident at her home in Topanga, California years later. Dora recounted the story: We felt the end of the world had come. Mama was gone. We were all alone. Now, this disaster had to happen. We felt it was our fault! Next morning father decided to search again, and there was our pet—what an irresponsible witch!—dining merrily in a patch of wild onions. How she managed to elude him is a mystery to this day. She was a fence-breacher and that's bad. But a good milker; her udder was so full it appeared ready to burst. Dad lead her home, dripping milk at every step. Happy children ran to fetch a bucket.

We sat down to enjoy late breakfast, so the story went. Cereal bowls glowing and tall glasses of heifer's-delight filled to the brim graced each setting. But alas! What was wrong? My sister drank a few gulps—frowned, then tested the oatmeal. That milk was terrible. Our best cow, who loved snacking on wild onions, had done an evil thing. We had fried eggs and potatoes for yet another meal.

Next day, the milk tasted better and our spirits revived. We kept a close watch on that heifer from that time on. Life taught us stern lessons in Cotterel:

> We wore button shoes, hand-muffs and shawls;
> Chalked names and dates on blackboarded walls—
> Happy girls in gingham—boys in overalls—
> Children's joys and sorrows ruled our play
> On any, most-unusual, yet "typical-ish" day
> Back in Cotterel valley—one octogenarian life
>   away.

TAMING THE WILD

Three eaglets lived in an aerie on a ranch framed against rising hills where mica sparkled on the rock and juniper boughs scented the wind. An historic castle would have been no more impressive than this ranch-house in the glade with a fine barn full of horses behind it.

They had all those mounts; all I had was one red mare. I rode there to gaze in wonder at the patchwork farms below. The sure-footed mare bore us two colts. One was spoiled with too many sugar lumps until brother finally broke him for his use.

The other got tangled in barb-wire:

His hind leg joint was slashed to bone
And three good legs were flawed by one.
He was the colt we nursed—poor brute—
The one dad finally had to shoot:
It was a dreaded, shocking thing
To watch that bullet strike and sting—
To see him wilt with failing breath—
We cried and willed his corpse to Death.

That was the end of our stringhalt horse when we saw he could not carry on, walking goose-step, making loud clatter on the wood bridge by the house. Our family was sympathetic to horses.

The eaglets referred to were actually three hardy brothers proud of being ranchers, and not valley farmers. I gazed at the cluster of buildings and wished I, too, were an eagle.

Whitefaced cattle grazed up the canyon, their muzzles splashed with a creamy white that matched the tones of limerock washed from the canyon wall. Wild sunflowers blazed in the sun, and Indian Paintbrush flamed red in the breccia by my feet. It was a place to hold picnics, I decided, and thought of those hard riding men wondering how they felt about their fortunate lot. One thing is very sure. They did not view their beautiful valley or the fine string of riding stock in the way I did.

The older boys had learned their lessons well. Beyond beauty or affection, a horse was simply locomotion. A whiteface steer roaming in the dew-wet morn never looked better than when butchered and hung from a pole in the freeze-time on a singletree lashed to a rope. The sound of coyotes brought no poetic response—they grabbed a thirty-thirty and chased them off.

The young brother had it much easier, and it reflected in his nature. He was not so dour or antagonistic. He was handsome, charming and quick to learn. The older brothers were determined to alter him. He proved a willing student when it came to expanding their exploits for he was as precocious as Billy the Kid. He learned to smoke and hoist the bottle with his elders without succumbing to the coarseness of his trainers. He enjoyed mixing with schoolmates and had many friends in spite of a reputation for wildness. Like his brothers, he could ride; and his mounts were choice.

Now we come to the sole incident for which this prologue was prepared. In summer, he worked with his brothers and soon could rope and brand like a man though tender behind the ears. The boys drove him hard. They saw that he took his turn at breaking in a new colt. He could raise the flask and drink right along with the rest, but his training in horse-breaking was incomplete.

Each morning the three saddled a green mount and the younger brother underwent a bucking spree while they cheered. This episode grew tiresome, especially one day when he was out of sorts and utterly disgusted with the slow progress being made in breaking one colt.

That evening, around the fire, he inquired of the experts present, "Just what do you do with a colt that gets too much dander in him every morning?"

"Easy," said one brother. "Be firm with 'im. Bop him a couple times if ya hafta! Show him who's boss, that's all."

The other conceded this was sensible, so they passed the bottle around again, spat in the embers of a dying fire and went to bed.

The very next day, the youngster decided to try the new advice. Sure enough, that colt decided to resist. With a bottle of liquor from the night before in one hand, the younger brother climbed aboard the obstreperous colt. The animal shuddered when he felt a weight, then came loose, crow-hopped and lunged right over the breakfast fire.

The youth, remembering his older brothers' advice, rapped the colt sharply on the head with his gloved hand--no help. Now, he rapped him again with the bottle; perhaps that would do the trick.

His brother should have warned him this was severe, but they were far from sober. They watched from the sidelines, shouting and cursing as pots and pans lay spilled around the fire from the first pass that outlaw made.

The kid was busy, but he managed to yell out of the side of his mouth, "What do I do now?"

"Hell!" shouted a thick-tongued voice from the sidelines. "Hit 'im again, kid! Clobber 'im." It was a wild sounding bellow.

"Yeah, boy! Hit 'im harder!" yelled the other. "Whoop-e-e-e!"

The rider did just that. He laid that bottle down

between the tender ears of that fine colt caught in peak of his jump with back curled in a bow and feet threshing at the ground like Pegasus alighting on Eden. What a shameful stroke! Those wild brothers should have paid dearly for that advice—perhaps in the final reckoning they will.

 Poor, beautiful, redcoated beauty—sleek of hide with glowing eyes filled with life and wisdom of the wild, fighting only to be free—struck down by a boy who could have just as well have been a lifetime friend.
 Beauty ended there, lying limp and broken. The mother who bore him suffered her pangs in vain. The stallion that sired him never saw him running free again, and the boy who transmitted a thoughtless blow was transported from innocence to murder at a stroke. Killing a man or a horse for no reason is beyond excuse.
 It is not a funny tale, nor is it pleasant to tell, but it pictures the mixed-up lives that marked an epoch of a time commonly called the Glorious Days of the Old West.
 Glorious or not—that beautiful colt was dead.

BASEBALLS AND HATCHETS

"Dismiss for lunch," the teacher called, and the entire school scrambled for the door.

Born Leaders: ROY with hat over eyes displays his independence.

In no time at all lard pails were opened and sandwiches gulped down. There was to be a ball game, and no precious time of this lunch hour could be wasted.

The heroine of this story, Aleatha, is a young lady who was reliant, resourceful and much to be admired. She wasn't homely

Little Pictures Portray Great Events: Roy's NEMISIS, gazing directly at camera, has look of self-assurance and good health. (Circa 1915, Cotterel School.)

or unattractive. She was a strong-boned fighter with a red strawberry mark that complimented her, for it set her apart as one girl who would stand her ground and ask no favors. Her sister, though of a different temperament, backed Aleatha if the need arose. Aleatha had an uncle who had been a major league pitcher. She and every student at the school heard those often-told stories about the baseball greats. Each

134

classmate believed baseball to be the game of sovereigns. It was constantly on their minds and in their hearts.

Roy and Aleatha were undisputed captains—sides were quickly chosen. Roy grabbed a bat and the rivals placed one hand above that of the other till they reached the top to see which side was first up to the plate. Roy's side won.

Forget if you can the unimpressive look of the surroundings, that bases were cowchips or a flattened remnant of a box, or a cast-off coat. Also overlook that fielders were short of gloves, bats were cracked and wrapped with friction tape, balls were lopsided and frayed in the seams. Nothing seemed quite right; but everyone knew how important the game was.

Play began in earnest as soon as bases were found and set and stray boulders cleared away.

There were boos and catcalls when the pitcher threw low, a loud wail when the batter struck out. The pitcher ground his heel in the dust, scowled at the batter, and the spitball thwacked into the catcher's mitt, just like in the majors.

Faces grew sweaty and taut as the game progressed; the strain of seesawing scores began to grind on everyone's nerves. A boy slid into home. "Out!" yelled the umpire.

"He was safe, the umpire is blind!" someone yelled.

"He was out—the catcher tagged him!" cried the opposition.

It seemed likely they would iron it out for a time; but, when someone found the scorekeeper was fouled up too, pandemonium reigned over all.

"That score is wrong!" yelled a captain. "Our man was safe and we won!"

"You did not—O, no you didn't win!" came a

strident female voice. "Your man was out, and we were even before that—so we won!" She stamped her foot and her team mates agreed.

Thus it began. A fist fight erupted between pugnacious Aleatha and hot tempered Roy, who was too mad to care who he was fighting. Aleatha met his flurry of punches head on, welcoming the battle, returning punch for punch—what a girl! The whole team joined the fray.

Cotterel School

A tattletale ran for the schoolhouse and the teacher came bounding. Her pleas of "Stop it, do you hear?" and "Don't you dare hit her!" were of no avail. She finally pried the ringleaders apart by sheer strength. The teacher tried to salve their wounded pride. She talked to both captains for a long time and strove to bring harmony to the battling teams.

Roy and his obstinate classmate would not apologize; so the teacher kept everyone after school. She said, "You will have to settle this quarrel or stay till you do!"

She asked different ones to give their version of the quarrel hoping to decide who was right or wrong but this attempt was fruitless. At last she had an inspiration. She brought out a hatchet and ordered the ringleaders to bury it—but the obstinate duo shook their heads. It appeared they were more willing to bury the hatchet in each other for neither wanted to apologize.

The teacher was baffled but determined. Backing down was bad for discipline in a one room school. Then another problem arose. Fall was here and dusk came early. What would the parents say? As for the students, no one relished the thought of stumbling through darkness down lonely rabbit trails to far-off dwellings. She had to give in.

"Students," she announced, "it is getting late and you have not cooperated; you had better go home; maybe tomorrow you will begin to see how foolish it is to quarrel like this."

She dismissed them with the summation: "The joy of any sport is playing the game fairly and squarely, not in arguing over who won!"

Roy and his stalwart competitor shook hands and made up the next day, but peace did not remain for long.

When my wife typed this story, she said, "Wouldn't it be strange if those two had finally married? There is a narrow dividing line between love and hate; such things do happen!"

All I could say was: "If they had married and a skirmish arose, I would hate to take sides with my brother against that girl with the spirit of a winner!" Fortunately for all of us it never materialized. Brother is laid to rest; and where does his rival dwell? I'll probably never know.

ROLLING UP THE WIRE

"Get up, Dwight," my brother called, "we're going to Cotterel to get some wire."

It was late October; crops were in, but snow had not yet arrived. We took some lunch, leather gloves and side cutter pliers and chucked them in the back of our cut down Ford and went belching down the road.

That old mover was a living wonder, spitting fire out of the manifold where the tailpipe gasket was gone. There was no muffler. The floorboards were nearly gone so you saw the fire and heat came up in blasts, along with noise and smoke.

In better days it had been a five passenger rig but the rear seat was cut away to make room for cargo. It steered like a wounded buffalo that lurched, quivered and jounced while your liver and spleen moved in all directions. My brother did pamper it when it fell sick and abused it unmercifully when all was working well. Luke was a man of contradictions, a stubborn fellow in many ways, and the Ford matched his personality completely. It loved to fume and haggle over brush and desert trails, endeavoring to toss us off and out like a range mustang would, but we both loved that old contraption. It tried to break the arm of whoever cranked it. When you were ready to swear it would not run again, after feverish cranking and yanking at the choke, it suddenly broke into fits of horrible coughing. This life-sign, when properly diagnosed in time with spark and choke, would level into steady sputters and then a loud-mouthed bellow.

We roared out to the dirt road and wound upward toward the foothills; then we veered east to open desert.

I had a guilty feeling when we parked that jalopy and began rolling up wire though most fences were down and the best posts had disappeared long before. The strands were rusty and loath to come out of weeds and earth. They had oxidized and grown stiff, sometimes brittle, but with a little care (and by dint of prying out loose staples and unkinking bent lines) we were able to salvage the wire. The original installers had long since gone-- their houses hauled away. Still I felt like a thief and trespasser with visions of a stern faced rancher confronting me with a shotgun. Luckily no one ever did.

We had lost our own shirt out on that selfsame strip and were probably as much entitled to these crumbs as anyone. Rolling the wire was an art. You built the coil by moving it right and left across the down wire, pulling it backward from time to time to tighten the roll and draw up any slack; if not, the loops would flop off and the whole thing was a scramble.

The barbs caught in your gloves and brought up thistles with them. You had to stop to untangle wires or loosen them from the stub of a post. By the time you had gone an eighth to a quarter of a mile the roll grew cumbersome and heavy. It was then, we cut the wire and started a new roll. It grew monotonous. I was twelve or thirteen; nevertheless, my brother saw to it that I was not overlooked when dull tasks arose. Whenever possible he would turn the whole thing over to me, but this was a two man job.

When we had assembled all the wires the back end would hold, we both lifted those heavy swatches of beastly-bristly up on the tonneau and the job was finally done.

Luke began to crank that old T-Model as I waited in hopeful suspense for the motor to respond.

Glory be! It started once more. As that aged jitney bounced and leapt down those sagebrush trails, we were both in great good humor by now with visions of home—an oil lamp glowing yellow on a loaded table. Dad, mother and sisters were all waiting to greet us and pass steaming bowls of food. Afterward, there was the promise of a warm fire in the living room while sister played the piano, and we read aloud and munched apples.

Sadness comes over me once again. Mother, father and both brothers are gone, and the wires we labored to collect have all rusted and fallen down. That was our Age of Innocence, end of "horse and buggy days." Though we rode in a car, we still used horses in the fields; we still had a coal oil lamp. Those were, "Mother needs some water in the kitchen" days.

Corn was sweeter on the cob, birds sang prettier, lilacs smelled sweeter and I ran at any excuse where I now walk with a cane. I never dreamed of seeing men on the moon, or envisioned freeways or Three Mile Islands. Men looked like men, girls looked like girls, and I was happy when dad handed me only a dime. So be it; those days are no more!

THE WHITE HORSE

One evening not long after the family arrived at Cotterel, a man rode up with a string of horses with the halter rope of one tied to the tail of the horse ahead. A horse best described as "mostly white" was next to last in the string.

The man rode right up to father and said, "Good evening, could I stay the night and put my horses in your corral?" No offer of money was made or expected for that was not the custom in those days.

"Sure," father replied, "Supper will be ready in half an hour. I'll tell my wife to put on another plate."

The man was of medium build and unshaven, and not the type you'd expect to see in any kind of trouble. He was dressed for the trail with an all-weather coat and a bedroll tied on the back of his saddle. No gun was in appearance; his gear had seen considerable service. He was fairly dark complexioned; that is all anyone remembered.

He was relaxed and talkative during supper, for Dad was a good host; the man enjoyed Mother's Swiss cooking. They talked of crops, weather and politics.

He bedded down by the horses. Mother cooked an early breakfast. By the time my sister woke, the man was leaving.

"Good-bye and good luck," Father said as he watched the man assemble the horses. Then he made an innocent observation. "By the way, if I were a horsethief, I sure wouldn't have a tombstone in my string. They're too easy to spot!" Father laughed at his pleasantry, and the stranger laughed too—a little, but he didn't overdo it.

Around mid-morning a car drove up the lane streaming a long trail of dust. Out stepped the sheriff. "Did you see anyone go by with about five horses. One of them was a white one?"

"Yes," Father answered. "Headed North, following ruts of the Oregon Trail right on the farm here. Next time I looked, the string of nags had disappeared. Figured he was headed for Snake River."

Not long after this incident our team disappeared; but that's another story. The sheriff asked a few closing questions and roared off in pursuit of a brash-but-foolish thief with a "tomsbtone" serving as fourth member of his band, trailing in his wake—and what a mistake.

As one clever tune relates: "It was a most unusual day."

Was he caught; did he get away?
No one I met knows.

JENNY AND THE GYPSY

PART I

JENNY

Bright sunshine streamed over the knolls near the Point when the covey of wagons came. Dust rolled in mushroom puffs; wood and iron creaked in rhythm to the clink of trace chains at the singletrees. A tall woman wearing a bright shawl drove the front wagon winding up the grade. She let the lines go slack, waiting for the first glimpse of a settlement in the valley. At last she brightened. "Take the lines. I see a farm house," she called in a foreign tongue to the husband dozing on a pallet at the rear.

Dressed in a rainbow of color with striking profile and inscrutable face, the woman minced past a loud-mouthed dog with a wagging tail and submissive expression. The woman paid him scant attention but studied the fat chickens digging in the yard, the well-kept farm tools. This was a good place to begin. She rapped decisively on the door panel and cocked her head to listen. When footsteps were audible, she steeled herself for the pitch.

A large-boned, confident looking farm wife answered her knock. The farmer's eyes widened at this bizarre visitor, but she concealed her surprise as best she could. Unflinching hospitality was taken for granted in early days on the homestead. A new face was almost always welcome. "Come right in," Jenny said to her unexpected guest.

The visitor knew exactly what to do. She displayed the proper amount of distress. Her voice sounded harsh and foreign as she said, "My babe-e-e is sick!"

Before her listener could respond, she

continued: "E-e-f you have a cow, the babe-e-e needs milk!" She looked ready to burst into tears.

"I'm sorry; I don't have any milk," the listener replied. Then her countenance brightened, and she smiled warmly at the visitor. I do have some coffee cake." That lady had a reputation for excellent cooking!

She stepped to the pantry and brought a generous helping of coffee cake in a tea towel along with bread and leftovers. The weather was blister dry, but they'd salvaged a small patch of veggies watered by hand from a cistern. She gave that visitor all the lettuce she could spare. The Gypsy received the treats with eager hands. They were long-fingered, deft and very brown.

"You are ver-e-e, ver-e-e gen-ner-rus—the-n-n-k you-u-u!" she said, then added, "Breeng me your pocket-a-book, and I blow good forshun e-e-n e-e-t! You be mi-te-e hep-py e-f-f I do-o!"

Though we call the settler's wife Jenny, that was not her true name. She declined the Gypsy's offer, for she wasn't superstitious or greedy. But the visitor seemed so disappointed, Jenny reconsidered. After all, it isn't every day a striking foreigner with a far-away, old-world face comes to your door and offers to brighten a humdrum morning by filling your near-empty purse with good luck. It would provide a new topic of conversation. How she needed that.

"Oh, very well," she said in resignation and surrendered her purse to the "giver" of spells.

The Gypsy lifted the purse carefully by a strap and held it far out from a capacious bosom. You could surely see there was no trickery or sleight-of-hand being used here, Jenny decided, watching every movement with rapt regard.

The spellbinder popped the purse open with her

thumb, drew a deep breath and pressed the opening to her lips. She blew in there a long time. Taut cheeks puffed, temples pounded, rushing blood tinted her face a deeper red. It was clear that Gypsy wished to inject a bagful of good luck in that threadbare purse as her thanks to the wonderful lady who kindly supplied tempting coffee cake and other treats. When this important task was done, the Gypsy snapped that blessed purse shut with a loud click and handed it back looking just the way it was before, except for one thing: a clinging scent of garlic now mingled therein, along with "good-fortune" so willingly offered and given.

The visitor did not want Jenny to open this purse right now. She gave a plausible reason. Gypsies know Americans are weak in alchemic science and spells, so she said, "Don't open now! Too soon—e-e-s Ba-a-d! Ba-a-d luck!" Then she departed.

The yellow dog barked-and-wagged good-bye till the woman disappeared from view.

Provisions were running low. The day was clear and bright. Jen's husband decided it was time for a trip. He invited the missus to enjoy a ride to Marshfield and stop at J. C. Murphy's Mercantile Store.

How many times had I gone there? Old Jim was a fine storekeeper with iron grey hair and he kept a tidy store. What a delightful place. Jim had any kind of stock, from gallon kerosene cans with a gumdrop stuck on the spout to stop the drip, to free crackers in a barrel by the stove. He had dry goods from gloves to overalls. The store held pungent odors of coffee and vinegar, raisins and turpentine. Mamie what's-her-name often sat on the counter, told jokes on town folks and greeted every newcomer with a wave and "Howdy doo!" Sometimes she sat in a creaking rocker and knitted as she talked. It was just like home. Folks sat around the stove and swapped news of the nation or just weather gossip. What nice folks they were.

When did Jen discover the Gypsy had done something unexpected that day? Guess is it was right after she stepped into Murphy's Store. Maybe you think the Gypsy put some extra money in the purse. I have to say the surprise was a little different than anyone expected. She hadn't told her husband a thing about the morning visitor. He would have said it was all nonsense, anyhow. Husbands just don't understand the women's world.

Well, she ordered some yard goods, flour, macaroni and what-have-you.

Then, her husband took his turn with a box of shotgun shells and ended with licorice for the kids. "Hand me your purse," he says, for she was boss in this family, and kept track of the money and the books.

Jenny does an unusual thing and hands him the purse. After all, she knows what he's doing. Its okay. He reaches in there and a puzzled look comes over his whiskers and face. He hands the purse back. She digs through the combs and cockamamie kadoo women carry in even small purses. (How they pack it in, I'll never know.) She rummages quite a while; dumps the whole thing on the counter and then light dawns.

The purse is bone dry! Not of junk—of money!

Of course, J. C. let them charge their purchases, but words came thick and hot for a time. That was the day a battle was fought in Murphy's digs and folks had their mouth open with surprise. Nobody butted in as the husband and wife sizzled and battled it out.

"What have you done with all our money?" the poor husband wailed.

At last his wife shoved him outside, for she was a strong woman who had no fear. She calmed him down, then spilled the whole short, quick story of a crafty Gypsy.

You can guess the rest. That husband, usually subservient, finally put his foot down. He told Jen what he'd wanted to say for years. He declared she was either incompetent or an idiot. He was petulant, *fretulant*, mean and overbearing. Perhaps, in the end, he realized losing that money was worth it. They quarreled and they argued-and-hated one another all the long buggy ride home. She never heard the last of it for a very long time.

PART II

BELLE

Now, if this were fiction, one episode would end it, but facts do not run on established plots; therefore, I'm compelled to continue.

That same brigade of dusty wagons wound on through the sagebrush searching throughout the settlement for food, clothes left on a line, anything of value not nailed down, watched or tended. A fat rooster—an unwary hen, a goat or enticing hog were all considered fair game, provided they left no track or telltale clue. Theft was honorable if you were not caught; stealth and clever deception were traits to admire, for vandals must live by their wits, not depending on brawn alone.

Afternoon shades began to lengthen when the tall woman with those piercing eyes doubled back on her trail and found a house setting back from the road yet to be tried. She prepared for her last foray that day.

By weird coincidence she knocked at the door of Jen's sister-inlaw who we will refer to as Belle, for I do not wish to anger posterity.

Belle was a fine, good-hearted woman, but her

cupboard like Old Mother Hubbard's was nearly bare at the time. Her husband was careful with cash.

By good fortune this family possessed a cow, and Belle gave the pleading Gypsy a half-gallon of milk, some precious radishes, and new potatoes.

The woman with expressive hands thanked warm-hearted Belle over and over. That Gypsy did a lot of waving and pointing in explaining her needs, and she got the point over very well. "I mus' do sum-thin' nize!" she exclaimed as she offered to make Belle's money grow. It was the selfsame schmoe!

Times were hard at Belle's place. This seemed the intervention of Fate, but she was no ignorant dummy. Perhaps she was just over-wishful and then she realized it was foolish. Belle pondered a time, finally replied, "No, thanks."

The Gypsy appeared very sad. After all, this offer was free, and she inquired what the lady had to lose?

At last the persistent Gypsy prevailed. There is precious little in there, Belle said to herself and handed the pitiless purse to hoping-hands. You know the rest. The Gypsy returned the purse to Belle with an easy-breezy smile. The spellcaster knew she was beyond suspicion. She grabbed up her gifts and fled. That's the last of her.

The owner, with relief and no suspicions whatsoever, crammed her purse back in the bedroom dresser. Her husband would arrive soon; it was time to fix supper, and that man was a real old bear if she was late. He was not easy to live with at times.

Belle never realized what had happened until Jenny, her sister-in-law, came for a visit. It was evident to Belle Jenny was upset or she wouldn't have come so near her last visit. What is up? Belle wondered.

Jenny broke the news in jigtime. "A Gypsy

cleaned out my purse," she lamented. "Did my husband tell yours?"

Poor Belle, the last to take the bait, didn't answer. Instead she rushed into the bedroom and returned with shaking hands. "My purse is empty too!" she groaned and burst into tears.

"Oh-h-h no-o-o!" Jenny blurted out in dismay. "What will your man say about that?" Both feared his caustic tongue.

You can well imagine how those husbands, two surprised brothers, reacted. How often that winter those two plotters, who seldom visited before this episode, got together as the storm howled outside, sharing new comradeship over cards and coffee, while their women smoldered and secretly cursed the conniving Gypsy who got away unscathed.

You my think this account is overblown. Well, you my not realize how just about *any* news could prove exciting in that tiny community in dead of winter. Everyone savored the tiniest morsel of gossip on a dreary day. It is possible that one of those two embattled wives my have spilled the beans (to use a tired cliché), for one of them was renowned as a blabber, though I dare not say more. But whether either divulged the secret makes little difference. The story did get out. Even the children of one couple heard the family ruckus and were sworn to secrecy—but you know children. Very soon the whole community was laughing in corners and whispering across the back fence until all was common knowledge.

The tale of that spellcasting, web-weaving Gypsy with the classic, old-world face and piercing eyes caught the imagination of almost every settler in the valley. It became one of the favorite folk stories of old Cotterel, and it would be regrettable if it moldered

150

into oblivion. So, after years of silence, those voices of the dryland, like an old gramophone playing in the dusk, can speak once more.

Did either of those two brothers attempt to track down the deceitful Gypsies to recover their money? It's just possible the discomfiture their wives suffered outweighed the money lost; both were contentious men. Whatever the reason, they did not pursue, and the Gypsy wagons trundled down the brushy trails headed for the shaded dells of a spectacular point on Old Oregon Trail beyond Massacre Rocks. There a picturesque campground awaited at Emigrant Springs along the Snake's meandering shore.

Here lay a scenic overlook where they could gaze on wild rapids, where great hawks soar above twisted cedars leaning over the brow of the cliff.

What a lovely place to fill with Indian teepees or buffalo herds, but the Indian dropped his moccasin and fled, limping to the reservation. The buffalo struggled and fell on countless hills; he bleached and blended with the dust in just such cul-de-sacs as these. So, the only substitute for wilderness that remains for us now is that far-off vision of Gypsy wagons camped above the streaming river with Gypsy music and song wending with the smoke, ascending to the stars one summer's night so long ago.

BLIND BARNS

I inquired of a young waitress at Grizzly Cafe in Burley where Cotterel might be. She looked at me with puzzlement. "Never heard of it," she said and went on taking the order.
"It's high time folks around here got some history moving," I said to my wife sitting next to me. "Maybe someone cares—someone remembers."
On to the courthouse we sauntered. A helpful searcher found Sam's town plat. I gazed in awe. There in large print it read: "Salt Lake and Idaho Railroad and Idaho-Pacific-Transcontinental Highway merging with Raft River Highway." They all came together on the main street of Cotterel. Spread before me Hubbard Baker and Wilson Avenue converged with First, Second, Main and Fourth streets bordering dozens of lots carefully platted. A cluster of mini-lots mince-stepped along the railroad's edge, undoubtedly zoned for commercial use. The railroad and highway ran catty-wampus through the scene.
Sometimes you get this *Alice In Wonderland* feeling when you find some unexpected image transposed over the familiar. I closed my eyes and tried to visualize this barren spot by the Point with an abandoned railroad grade fading by the year, a tumbleweed mound running aimlessly for miles. Here a few rusty strands of 'bobwire' dither and fret with no task or excuse where busy trains once tooted. Rails and ties are gone; not a chimney remains to loft signals skyward, reminding me of a ghostly mining town named 'Skid-doo' we visited on a Death Valley trip long ago.
Stand on a bluff; shards of glass, shining in the sun, pinpoint boundaries of each departed roof—a desolate sight. Silence implodes; ol'-man-wind whistles

through unseen lips as you study this dreary spot. Is that who it is? Or is this a passing shadow with one measly blanket and a bony burro? You look again and dismiss the whole—vague signs of a pending sunstroke—not a lizard stirs.

Meanwhile, at Cotterel, amid rubble and clods, we spy shards of a grain drill—a desolate foundation slinks in a copse of tumbling-mustard weeds.

My father arrived here in 1914. My sister, May, remembers when the first steam cranes arrived at the Point digging a cut through dense lava and continuing onward to Idahome. The curve at Cotterel was sharp; U.P. locomotives whistled; laboring wheels 'squeakily-complained' to stubborn rails as train bells tolled.

I think of Hemingway's title, 'For Whom the Bell Tolls.' That Cotterel train bell, one of my whimsical illusions, should have intoned:

"Get out of Cotterel! You're not welcome!"

The grain elevator was built in 1917 by C. C. Baker, an insurance agent at the time. Mr. Baker died at 102 years of age. That's worth a mention. Settlers were either gone or near to leaving at the time of completion.

Above, two recalcitrant towers mope—frozen here over three quarters of a century—a bit Sphinx-like to a child's imagination. Each of those two cement columns had a series of doors that could be opened all the way to the top. The doors are gone—so is the roof; the sturdy towers are pitted by gunfire of hunters and vandals passing through. They are tall stacks; in the upper crannies, pigeons nest and make pleasant, cooing sorties.

Perhaps some feckless gopher, desultory pheasant or ragged coyote comes this way. Few visitors linger, but small cottontails enjoy safe-haven in rocky batholiths nearby.

Sam's store and post office saw busy times here. His home stood quite near where a grade crossing marker once stood. Pauline and I found shards of violet bottle glass and traces of mortar from a chimney there.

Above, the mountain broods. In the mid-nineteen-hundreds, a fire started on the west slope of Cotterel mountain and stripped the summit clear to the rim-rock cap on the eastern rim.

A once-thriving settlement is mere-history now; no chimneys, no malls, a jumble of stubble and clods. This tract was platted by a surveyor at Sam Cotterel's request. Now, twenty pigeons comprise the steady population—and who gives a coo or a hoot?

There are ghosts in Cotterel. Perhaps they care.

My sisters often gazed on those towers while tippling at hopscotch or skipping rope on recess at Cotterel school. Since those unenlightened years many changes ensued. Many of those abandoned farms have been reclaimed. Powerful electric pumps irrigate fields of alfalfa and grain. Last I heard our dry-tract homestead of the old time is now a dairy.

There is no need for a city here; none exists. Fast cars race down modern highways to Declo, Rupert or Burley when a need arises.

My oldest sister, whose years on this globe far exceed my own, has excellent recall of life at Cotterel. "Mother expected me to help with the housework. One distasteful chore was 'turning' butter. We didn't ever call it churning. I kept pumping the handle of that big gray crock but nothing happened. Mom was gone; so, with no one to advise me, I kept working until my arms ached. I thought mother would blame me for not following orders. At last, she came up the trail with a waggy-tailed dog right behind her.

"'Didn't you know you need cooler cream than

this to make butter?' Mama shook her head as she said this and opened the churn. Within lay a sorry-looking gray mess and no butter at all." May smiled at the memory. "That's just one of many things we learned out there on the dryland. You'd never find that out when you buy it in the store."

She recalled another time so remote now: "I think I was in the third grade when the teacher excused us to walk to the railroad cut-and-grade to watch the road crew lay curving rails around the Point. There was a crew of men on each side of the track. They had a 'loco' with a flatcar. There were actually four flatcars on site with rails-and-ties, and barrels of spikes. We stood on one side and watched the men lay about two lengths of iron ribbon. The last thing I remember is how good white-and-pink peppermint candy tasted that day—another fleeting memory of Cotterel."

In the stony gullies of that railroad cut, right near the Point May just mentioned, my brother, Roy, indicated a particular spot; many years had passed. "Here," he said, "right under your shoe soles are actual remnants of the Oregon Trail. Steam cranes excavating a deep trench through lava beds lifted huge rocks and piled them a crane-boom length from the track below. Ranchers found these behemoths too heavy to budge, so this strip was never plowed or farmed. Ancient wheel-and-hoof impressions, with these big rocks scattered anon, grow dimmer every year. Those crane-men, without thinking, saved a little piece of history and hardly anyone is aware of it."

It is interesting to note many other spectral trails lie in adjacent sands; one is the California Trail. Cassia County Courthouse tract books clearly show these ancient roads; so we have permanent records of them. Tourists of today have little time to worry over wagon ruts and other fading landmarks.

On my last visit in the 1990's, we drove to Cotterel directly after a stop at the courthouse in Burley where I viewed and copied several maps. My wife and I gazed, one more time, on scenes of an old fiasco. I felt 'spirits' about, heard echoes, saw visions—reviewing scenes of horses and wagons, tassel-topped buggies and early automobiles jouncing down desert trails. Names like Quanstrom, Genes and Mueller come to mind. Jack Gribble, a bachelor-neighbor, was a friend of Luke, my brother.

The Schrenk children, a host of them, a big family—the Hausens, Mitchells, Kulms, Bemers, the Skaggs family (founder of Safeway), and many others were whispering in the shadows. Was that merely a breeze brushing my cheek? Old men grown lonely for past faces bestir and return to scenes of childhood. Two hours passed.

We drove to Malta. How persistent black flies are. There, where a desert dump simmered in the sagebrush—and not a soul was about—tangled strands of Hiram Scutt's Arrowplate Barb begged to be rescued from oblivion. I stopped. That's a fetching wire for display boards. Cleverly stamped from sheetmetal, this barb with an Indian motif was considered a showy, decorative top wire to place around lawns and gardens of 1880's farm homes. They made the arrow barb look handsomer by adding a one-inch square wooden block here and there, now ain't that a show; but there's another reason.

You see, early day range cattle and horses gamboling free and unfettered tangle themselves in barbwire with dire consequences, especially at night. That is why a wooden block was woven in the lines along with the barb to catch the roamer's eye and make it veer away; it was a good idea right after they fenced most open range (this wooden block was an invention of H. B. Scutt).

    We circled back to Declo. Claude Vallette was walking in his wife's iris garden when I arrived. Wilma, a gifted pianist and artist, once tended a world-famous collection of iris bulbs. She is gone from this vale. Claude had been quite ill, the year before; he was improving when we met. It gives me a tug-and-lift to see him smile on this visit. He has remarkable flair for threading a story, a sharp wit and sound memory. Now he feels the weight of a lonely house, a weedy garden in ruins. He was a generation ahead of my pen, a carpenter who worked with my oldest brother, Roy.

    Inside the house he'd built when the family was small, shelves of books crossed an entire wall. I sat in there and remembered when Wilma drove mother and me to a Ladies' Aid meeting. I was but a tot then. It was the first 'enclosed' car I'd ever seen; now I was riding in one. Imagine that! It had 'real' doors with 'true' glass windows that rolled up and down with a crank. It even had a heater! Up to that time, cars simply had isinglass[1] curtains. I enjoyed that trip with Mrs. 'V' who'd easily learned to drive. Lots of women never tried that. There was a skift of snow and we sat in sweet comfort in the shelter of our new automobile.

    The Vallettes were undergoing a period of good times. They had a farm directly south of our boundary. That was before they moved to Declo.

    What a pleasure it was to go over to their place with a big barn and a long grove of poplars to climb. My sisters hung May baskets on their door; knocked

---

[1] Closed cars were permanently secure. Before that time cars were drafty. To make them more snug in winter we used attachable, flexible window curtains of 'isinglass,' manufactured from fish bladders. Those 'mountable' curtains were secured by iron rods sunk in the car's door panels. In summer, we removed the curtains entirely.

and ran. My brothers went along. Mr. Vallette came hustling out, spotted those baskets and decided to have some fun. It didn't take long before he searched and corralled them in the barn loft.

"Come on out! " he ordered, waving a big stick.

My kin, especially my small sisters were alarmed; you were not expected to be caught on a furtive, knock and run, wild May Basket Night. It wasn't supposed to happen!

Well that big chap had them at bay—two small girls and a couple surprised boys were collared by Claude and his Napoleonic-resemblant brother, Jean— slated for 'high' trials at Vallette's kitchen court. Wilma greeted them; she too, enjoyed a bit of nonsense now and then.

Soon, the terrible head-jailer, relenting slightly, dispensed warm cocoa and cookies, and insisted his penant-miscreants should dutifully think about their vagrant ways. Then he wound up the gramophone—or was it a Victrola?—and encouraged them, very politely now, to down more treats? On top of the spinning record, they were thick in those days, Wilma placed a wooden figure doing a clog dance on the turntable. How could it do that? I saw it myself, another time. Point one is: it didn't take much to entertain children in those days. Point two: you can surely see they were stern folks back in the twenties!

In addition to furnishing us two oil paintings that once hung on our wall, Wilma prepared a remarkable genealogy of the Vallette family; now, her inquiring, inspiring spirit is gone from our land. Little did she know I would write her epitaph. The people you meet from day to day, weave you into the tapestry of their lives; and, in so doing, change you forever, We reflect the people we emulate.

Back to Claude in a house now deserted. We're

seated in the spacious living room this skilled carpenter had also filled with love for his family. He liked both my brothers. Memories drift in as I write. He is speaking of my family now:

"Droz's moved off the Cotterel tract in 1917. I think that's right because we bought a farm from uncle Harry in 1916—first crop was 1917. Roy Droz, was twelve or thirteen years old then. I had barley to cut, but a colt kicked me and the wound caused an abscess. Austin came and unloaded one load of barley and didn't try to stack it. He left. Roy came bright and early next day and we started hauling barley. Just got it in the stack, and the threshing machine man said, 'Be here in the morning.' Robert Droz was bagging on the thresher that day. He would take one more stitch than Smothers—that made Smothers mad."

We laughed at this historic bit of scrap. I reminded Claude my father was a miller's son. How many times had he stitched a bag of grain? A good many.

We talked about Declo citizens I knew and what had happened to them in years that followed. More faces came to mind. I asked about John Hill, the indestructible blacksmith, and about Ollie Anderson and his brother, that amazing chap with a hare-lip—Bill, no less. We spoke of Carl P. Kennedy, the soft-spoken druggist, a famous man in Declo. I inquired about the Parke boys, the Bauers and Gillettes. Jimmy Murphy was a storekeeper friend of mine. If I didn't talk about him, I should have. His shelves held yard goods, spices, overalls, canned peaches and coal oil lamps, together with penny candies—all that in the realm of a small country store. There, sitting on top of Jim's front counter, plying knitting needles, lounged Mamie Boyer, his son-in-law's wife, garrulous, gossipy, laughing Mamie with a heart of gold.[1]

My visit with Claude brings all these people to mind. You will pardon me if we missed mention of a few of them, reviewing my years at Declo. I'd gone far afield, after that. Claude had remained. We looked back together at the foibles, fortunes and failures life had meted out both to us and our friends. A thousand stories lie here and 'C. V.' could have furnished many. Hank Anderberg called about then; he wanted my host to join him at the Cowboy Cafe right on the edge of Declo. This was a ritual he and Claude re-enacted frequently. I went along. It was the last time he and I shared memories.

At the Cowboy Cafe, I saw many strangers and a few folks I recognized. Just then, in walked Ivan Schrenk and his son. Ike looked big, weather-beaten and hearty as ever, the one man who'd known me at Cotterel and years after. He knew my brothers, my entire family. What a small world it seemed. A stretch of years 1915 through 1981 we bridged in about an hour. The coffee was strong and hot.

I mentioned to Ike how dad's horses were stolen. I told him how dad searched all over Cotterel and was getting desperate, and that our nearest neighbor came to our house and said: "Droz, you're going at it all wrong. See Sam Cotterel immediately!" He assured my pop that Sam, town postmaster and storekeeper, had more savvy about what was going on than anybody else in the whole town. 'S' had several sons active in the community, too.

Dad went to him and talked about his problem.

---

[1] *Declo, My Town, My People* (Declo, Idaho Historical Committee, 1974), p. 5, reads: "Jimmy Murphy who ran [the store] with the help of his son-in-law, Lew Boyer…, who with his wife Mamie… lived in the back of the store. Why don't they simply say Mamie is Jimmy's daughter? That's how I consider it."

"I'll look into it right away!" was all Sammy ever said.

Dad hadn't dug up one clue. We were literally ruined without that duo. A morning or two later, our team re-appeared like magic, tied to the gatepost of our corral; this gave dad the courage to strive on.

Ike remembered the theft well. We mulled over suspects. He figured Mr. X or Mr. Y knew something about that heist. I'd kept tabs on some of those settlers after we moved from Cotterel to Declo. (Ivan, or Ike, his nickname, was a goldmine of facts on Cotterel. He owned a lot of acres there including one tract where the Mark's well was located. We drew our water from what eventually became Schrenk's well. It was 300 feet straight down with a windmill whirling overhead. Idaho has a lot of wind, thank God, or we'd have gone bone dry.)

Anyway, there was an active horse stealing operation functioning freely in Cotterel. Ivan was quite aware of the problem, and it was on two occasions we talked about "Blind Barns." On one interview he mentioned that Family X—I'll not divulge the name this late in life—in fact, "lived off the land." They stole a team of bays and a bald-faced horse, stole them with the harness on. Two bays were sent to Portland; the bald-faced nag was returned all the way from Wyoming.

Ivan stated specifically: "There was a blind barn located in Cotterel, somewhere near the Point. Marshall Perrins worked for Sam Cotterel. It is possible a blind barn was located in an outlying area beyond his holdings. Details are unclear as I write; no accusation is involved. We merely clarify a specific area thieves may have utilized.

Ivan mentioned there were blind barns at Rockland and another at Walpi. He said there are still signs of rock corrals in that area. I'm a mite uncertain on the authenticity of two additional locations, but here they are for some historian to check out. Ike Schrenk said a ring of horse thieves was operating at the time dad lost his team. He mentioned other spots, also. One sounded like DeMurry the second was Marshall Springs. Both had 'blind' sites where horses could be hidden from prying eyes. Ivan stated blind barns were part of the reason horse thieves were so successful in our area. They were often well-managed 'dug-aways', important when travelers were about. Poles and brush shielded them from spotters on the rim-rock.

Thieves trailing through Cotterel often crossed Snake River at Bonanza Bar, entered Black Mesa—a wild spot!—and continued on to northern Idaho.[1] That route was actually an international channel, and well organized. Stolen horses were collected as far away as Utah and sold well away from the place they were stolen. Pattern was: Steal them in Utah, collect and sell more, a few at a time, as you hit for Canada. Conversely, Canadian horses were pooled there when you arrived. On return trips, you sold them as you tailed for Idaho, then back to Utah—a round trip ticket.

Today, thieves have car theft rings, so what is new?

Cotterel, a hamlet few remember. It burgeoned like a fat mushroom following the rain, blanched in awesome heat, just as we were, and vanished without a trace. Soon we Cotterelites will all be gone. Will those two stark towers remain much longer?

My last visit with Ivan was a short one. A few of his family still remember me and we share his

---

[1] DeMurry is how I taped this. I couldn't find it in an Idaho Atlas. Time will tell. Blind barns existed. How many? Who know.

memory. There is no forest on the rim-rock to mention, and only the wind knows the ways we trod, but the wind never says—just whistles and moves on. Farewell, old settlers. We will join you soon. Meanwhile we write and remember the good days when furry-leafed 'pinks', like fairy rings, were sunning in the sage.

FLIGHT FROM COTTEREL

Homesteads once filed upon must be earned. Up went pole barns lined with wire, filled with thistles or straw to cut off the biting wind that whined in the eaves with teeth on edge, tearing at your coat, blowing sand or powdered snow in your eyes.

Sheds were topped with brush, straw or willows, whatever was available.

As Matthew Arnold penned:

> "Pomona loves the orchard;
> Liber loves the vine,
> And Pales loves the straw-built shed
> Warm with the breath of kine...."

And so did we. Listening to the sound of feeding cattle, glad to be out of the storm. There were few good shelters in those lean years—a few sparse and ravaged clapboards, nailed to posts, partially cut the wind. There was too much to do and too little time.

Get up the frame and put a roof on the house. Rail the land, clear off lava rock, dig the cistern, cut brush for the fire—prodigious piles of it. Ten miles to Marshfield for a few groceries and coal oil for the lamp—but where's the money? Somebody's sick—where's the medicine? Ride to the neighbor or travel to a doctor. But it's snowing—there's a blizzard coming.

The buggy wheel's broken; a horse is down with colic. The cows broke out; they aren't anywhere in sight! I need to do the washing and we're out of water. Roy, go to the Mark's place; the cistern's dry. Looks like it's hailing. Who left the henhouse door ajar? A weasel broke in last night—five chickens are dead. And so it went—on and on—pioneering!

First, a shack or tent. Next, clear the land, plow and plant. Priorities, drudgery, and unremitting work. It pains me just to think of what it must have been. I was too small to be counted, but it's all there in my mind like the flashback of a frontier movie.

Our effort to create Eden on the desert was short-lived. We began near the end of a wet cycle uncommon to that land. The grubbing-rails tore the rich soil, the plows creased it into furrows and wheat rolled in green waves across the flatland that first virgin season when the promise was rich and Nature smiled, but the devil bided for time in the wings.

Old Satan grinned and watched us prod our straining teams as we cleared away brush and rock and strung fence lines in a rush of strain and sweat.

Then, as wheatlands rippled and we sang songs of thanksgiving—that very year, disaster waited—as the poet put it well: "Then, the weather turned around!"

Next year was a dry cycle—faces turned grim. The wheat stem withered and the wind rolled clouds of sand. The grasshopper, rabbit, and gopher had multiplied when food was plentiful; now, they swarmed out of the desert and into the fields, stripping what greens remained.

How suddenly it changed with that sinister twist of weather. New-built dwellings would be abandoned—left to rust in the sun, their shingles curled and rattled in the hot, unceasing wind.

On Mark's place, years later, a windmill—once

the pride and joy of every settler around—was left in ruin. The brake no longer held, and the "mill" ran amok till it's pump-rods threatened to strip away; blades spewed from the untended wheel to lie, like prehistoric shards, across the blistered earth. Three hundred feet below was crystalline, sweet water. Above lay thistles, seven-year locusts braying in a bush and naked sand.

Drought, dust and tumbleweeds were all that remained.

This was often the scene: The worried farmer hung on, hoping for a miracle. Perhaps it would rain. He delayed long after time for prudent departure. The men who labored with undiminished zeal and sacrifice, pouring sweat and tears on this unresponsive soil finally arrived at that fateful day of exodus.

This last day started like any other. Haggard men rose somber eyed, picked listlessly at the dwindling food and stepped outside pretending to start work as usual. In that moment they viewed the desolation of their fields, mulling over debris and bitterness of shattered dreams. Wandering out to the straw-barn to observe the horses with gaunt ribs, chuffing on a few stems that remained, whinnying for a fresh forkful of alfalfa that was non-existent, the farmer suddenly came to his senses.

Leave it, now! Leave it all, forever! Give it back to the plaintive dove, the stalking coyote wailing on the rim-rock, the wily rabbit who, unlike man, subsists on the dew of a desert morn and whatever else he may glean. Leave it to crow, hawk or owl deep in his burrow, to the roaming nighthawk who sweeps the gnat from the sky at dusk, waking desert ghouls with the sound of his booming wing.

This land was made for primitives, not men in faded overalls and tattered shirts who need swollen fields, live streams, and fenced corrals for their mares and foals where the terrain is benign.

And so they prepared to run. Disillusioned, sad, sick and worn, they gazed into the red dusk or stood under the glittering milky way, staring at unrepentant heaven with a rush of fear knotting their stomachs, torn with half-joy at leaving, running in coward's retreat to a better place and better time.

By morning the hastily-gathered gear was packed. The wagons bristled with hoe, broom, crock, blankets, pillows and a child's bauble or two. Then, handing up the wee ones who disappeared sleepily over the back of the tailgate, the settler and his sad wife clambered to the spring-seat.

The deserter, now migrant, clucked to the gaunt grey and the cocklebur-tailed bay and they jounced off between low-running tiers of Russian thistle headed for the rutted swales of the Oregon Trail that skims through wash and coulee to the Point. There, the wagoneer dropped wheels into the lime splashed lava cut and headed due west for Marshfield.

A crate of jabbering chickens objected beneath the spring-seat while a disconsolate cow braced and tugged on a rope strapped to the wagon reach.[1]

It was common practice to carry essentials only—the first trip out—like pots and pans, bedding and staples. Leaving in haste, the settler left heavier furnishings and farm tools to pick up the next time around. The urgent consideration was not goods and chattels. It was simply this question: Where will I find a roof for my family and a way to exist?

So the farmer urged the horses into a swinging trot when terrain allowed and promised his wife he would go back for the furniture, the quilting frame and

---

[1] Perhaps he dropped that cow off at the nearest neighbor's place and got someone else to trail her to Marshfield.

a spare bed grandpa once carried across the plains—hoping they would be settled soon. Then the nightmare would be over. They headed for the irrigation project west of Cotterel with beating hearts, longing to restock their dwindling supply of food, scrub the desert sand from their bodies and bathe in a cool canal. When the tardy settler finally returned to the homestead for another load, he received a shock. Vandals had stolen the plow, sacked the rooms, and emptied every chest and drawer. They had shattered every windowpane and hauled off entire buildings. Those poltroons turned over pump organs and caved in their backs or carted them away. Our own house stood naked, gaping through sightless windows. The door was pried open and swung in the wind. Clothes and books lay pilfered and strewn in a way that brought tears to our eyes and an ache to our hearts. My sisters rushed to the attic to reclaim one big rag doll named Geraldine. Eureka! She survived.

It was over and done. For us the sun would no more rise like a great yolk of yellow gold on the rim of eastern hills. The roving nighthawk would never entertain us again in this savage land. The grey owl's soft lament would never float down through purple dusk across those haunted ridges. The furtive rabbit would no more test our will to shoot.

The sagehen could raise her brood unmolested and the tumbleweed would multiply and feast on the fields we left. The rattler and badger could inhabit the tunnels of our root cellar with impunity.

The coyote was again master of the ridge, and the golden eagle could enjoy the freedom of ample sky without fearing the settler's gun. The only train of emigrants left to weave over this land was a row of high-banked clouds marching overhead. Dust drought and death lingered there, hoping we would return.

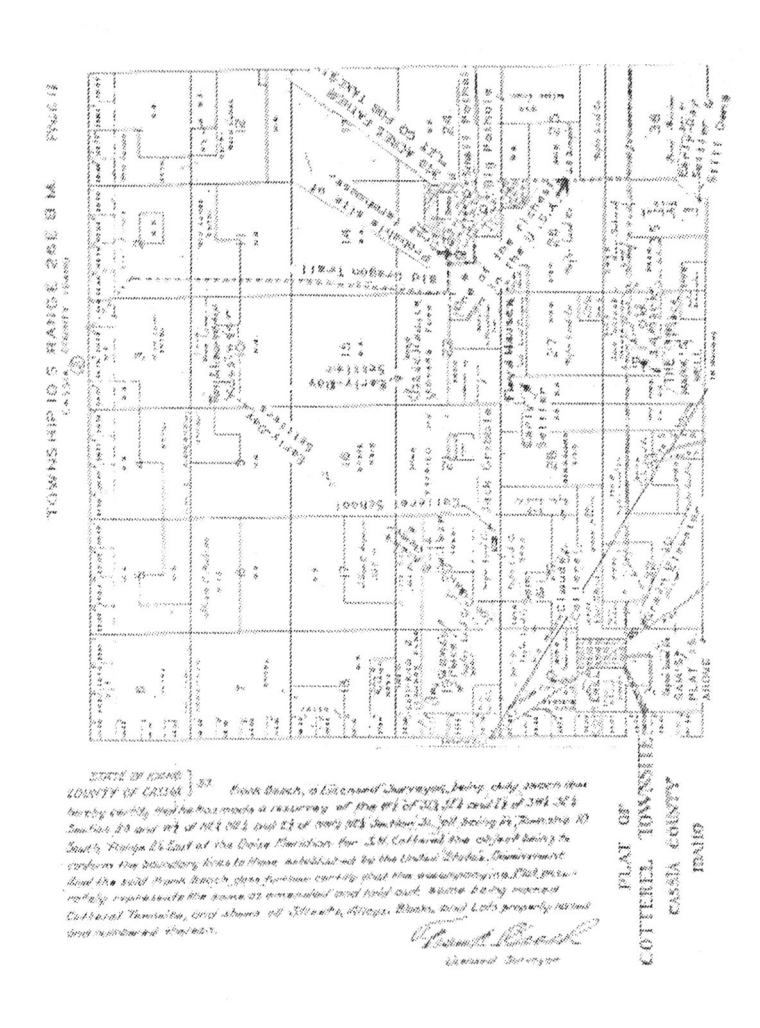

Plat map of Cotterel Township (Township 10 S Range 26E B M), Cassia County, Idaho. Walk a mile down a road and you pass by four 40-acre tracts. Note, section south of Droz land was owned by Jack Simplot, "The Potato King." At the bottom left corner is the town of Cotterel with remaining two grain elevators.

A PLAT, A TOWN, A DREAM

Sam's dream of Cotterel lies like a pressed blossom absentmindedly tucked away in one of those ancient books at Cassia County Courthouse. That site is a lonesome derelict today and looks more desolate since a fire depleted the cap of the mountain above. The fire started on the Dewey side, the west side of the Cotterel Mountains, and trailed over the top till the junipers were singed all the way across. Those groves were a shamble the last time I visited the area. Squinting skyward, all I could see were lava caps and puff clouds drifting over. Below, where the talus ends, lay summer-fallowed grain fields and two ghostly towers. Joined like Siamese twins, these white cement stacks are all that remained to indicate there once was a settlement here. Alas, I am one of only a few who remembers a hamlet called Cotterel.

"Well, it's going to be a great place," said a newcomer, staring out of the postoffice window!

More fool us! Today there are green fields and irrigated land further down the valley, but the old townsite is deserted. Declo is the next community. That sloping land alternates between years of rippling wheat and seasons of brown stubble and it is still a dry farm area. The mountain chain actually starts here. Visible for miles, the northern tip of a promontory that settlers named "The Point" rises North of those elevator stacks. Old "prof" Rodenbaugh, a septuagenarian, dry and slim as a climbin, stick, lectured us In Pokie's (Pocatello's) "Southern Twig" about this thrust fault that unravels the Cotterel mountains as they shinny off toward Utah.

At one time this was level plain. While volcanoes poured layers of chocolate lava over the land, internal stresses ruptured the pie plate. The west side lifted; the east side dropped. A mountain scar hove in view. Those lava-capped top layers require ropes in many places to gain the summit.

My oldest brother who knew so many of the old timers, trapped the rim rock for coyotes and bobcats. More than once, a golden eagle fluttered in the jaws of a Victor trap, lured by bait for other prey.

Like that eagle, Sam "C", and each of us, was trapped in Cotterel's empty promise. Fate and demigods of bad weather sat in shadowy robes high in those juniper crags and smiled icily at proceedings where men labored and destroyed what beauty there was. Toothed winds chewed the dust on newly-plowed fields. Thirst and a withering sun conspired against us.

> How often with my sorrel mare
> I rode up from the desert, bare,
> To where the rim rock lava thrust
> Surmounted by the acrid dust,
> While bright and pouring sun peered down:
> The wild sunflowers milled around
> As my mare climbed the rim rock steep
> To view the valley, fast asleep;
> And distant water shimmered far,
> Or glistened like a vitriol star
> Where junipers, those gnomes of Pan,
> Stood, dwarfish figures of a man.

I asked a youthful waitress in a Burley restaurant where Cotterel might be found. This was in 1985. She shook her head vaguely and smiled. "I've never heard of it," she replied.

Few Burleyites remember; and, for that matter, I'm suspicious that many Decloans know much of Cotterel history. Only a handful of old timers remember the settlers and the failure and the exodus.

Pauline and I drove out to the Point that

171

afternoon and stood by the towers. I surmised we were near the base of Hubbard Avenue. "There is nothing here but scraps of metal from a farmer's grain drill, wood shards and rubble where the railroad ran," I said to my wife.

We stared at the sole remains of Sam's town. Sam's plat lay in the northeast quarter of Section 31, Township 10S, Range 26E, Boise Meridian, Cassia County. It was slashed diagonally by the 200 foot right of way of Salt Lake and Idaho Railroad plus an adjoining strip about 40 feet wide planned for the Idaho Pacific Transcontinental Highway that left the railroad and headed east on Main Street near the center of the plat.

If you think this chapter of Depression history is mainly concerned with property descriptions let me put your mind at rest. We are interested in the lives and times of human beings on a vanished frontier. Nevertheless, I've taken a moment to describe where Cotterel sat simply because it is one of these unique places named on a map that completely disappeared, a railway, elevator building and, post office, store and dwellings. All are gone.

At one time this town contained Wilson, Baker, and Hubbard Avenues plus First, Second, Main, Third and Fourth Streets—so says Sam's Plat of Cotterel Townsite of May 1917, surveyed by Frank Beach. Where did it all go? Down the wind, banished in dust and ashes, that's where. Nevertheless, there sits the plat map firmly locked in the aging courthouse tract books, yellowing slightly decade by decade. As we said, Sam established a post office in Cotterel the year I was born, 1912. At the time he did this, we lived in Kansas. That busy clock that wrings its hands over my escapades contrived its own dilemma for me when it let my path cross Sam Cotterel's. Still carried in my parent's arms, I

172

do not remember seeing him or his post office and store. I'm sure he saw me. I met many old settlers after we departed Cotterel—our homestead. The Schrenks, Bemers, Hausens, and so many others, held great expectations for this raw track.

Living in the green belt of Washington's Puget Sound, I find myself wandering back to Cotterel. Driving up the lane to Dewey Ranch, I never get out and introduce myself; I would be just a stranger to them. I motor around the Point and stretch my legs at the elevator spires. It all seems so inaccessible, now. That land was wide open when Sam held sway. The fences came soon enough, but you could find roads and trails everywhere. Although settlers were leaving, Sam hung on. The Plat of Cotterel Townsite was of little use by the time surveyor, Frank Beach, finished it. The plat date reads May 1917 and that was too late! Even at that point in time, there was evidence of trouble brewing. Cotterel was done for!

COTTEREL

Cotterel Post Office (Property Description): northeast section 31, township 10 south, range 26 east, of Cassia County, Idaho; 9 miles east of Declo; 16 miles northwest of Malta. Established: July 8, 1912, Samuel H. Cotterel, postmaster. Jennie I. Fimpel, postmistress, September 10, 1913. Claude D. Cotterel, postmaster, December 27, 1915. Discontinued: December 31,1917. Mail redirected to Idahome.

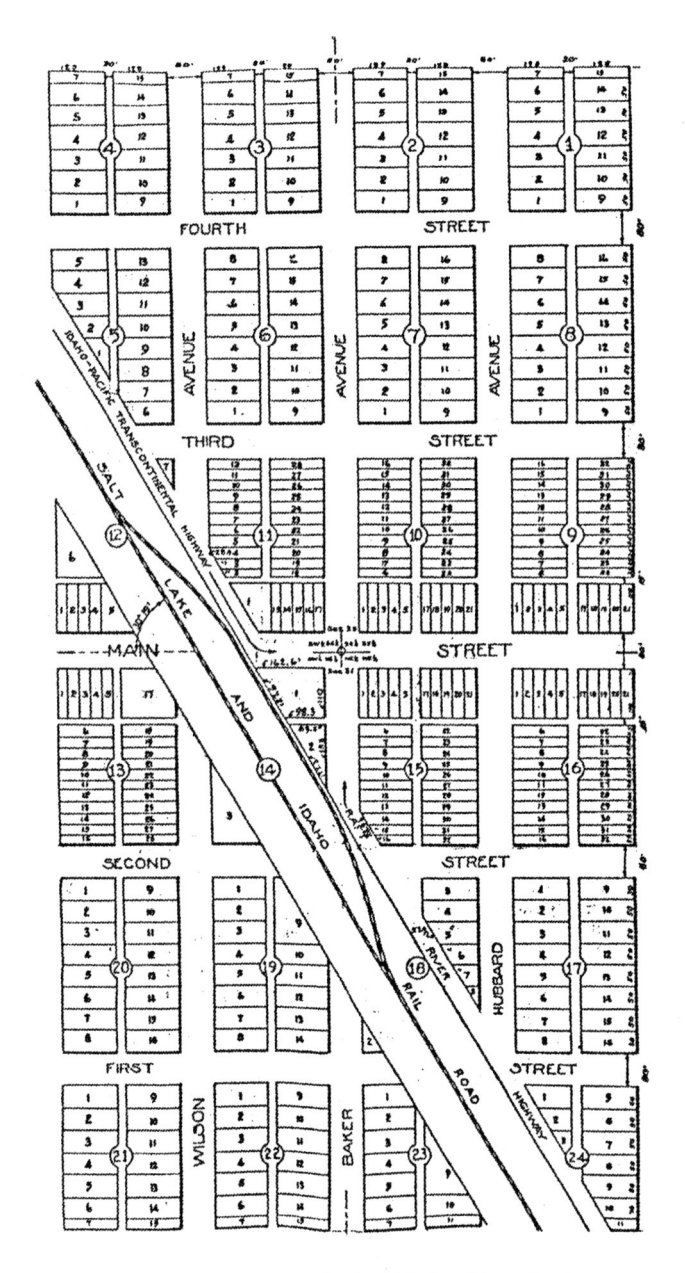

Plat map of Cotterel. Today this land is a dry farm.

174

Two linked grain elevator stacks. All that remains of Cotterel.

The mountain behind (east of) the twin elevators is "The Point," an impassible ridge of black basalt.

Bibliography

Declo—My Town, My People. Compiled by the Declo History Committee under sponsorship of the Declo Alumni Association: Margaret Clayville, Wilma L. Vallette, Vera C. McBride, Genevieve Olsen, Teresa Parke, Welton Allen, Louise Zadorozny, LeRoy Darrington, Cleone Moncur, Joseph A. Gillett. Burley, Idaho: The Burley Reminder, Inc., 1974.

Glover, Jack. *The Bobbed Wire Bible, VI.* Sunset, Texas: Cow Puddle Press, April 1980.

Grover, David H. *Diamondfiled Jack: A Study in Frontier Justice.* The Lancehead Series, Nevada and the West, 1968.

Howe, William H. *The Butterflies of North America.* New York, 1975.

"Culture on the Cuff"

LITTLE BLUE BOOK NO. 94
Edited by E. Haldeman-Julius

Trial and Death of Socrates

Edited, with an Introduction, by
Lloyd E. Smith

E. Haldeman-Julius, 1919-1951
Little Blue Books
(actual size)

Culture on the Cuff (Contents of Volumes One Through Four)

1. Introduction
Preface
Author's Introduction
The Idaho Trek

Two Tales My Barber Told Me
Where The Dreaming Lamplight Glows
1. The Gifted Barber
2. Kalispell Hop

People, Skits, and Cheesy Bits
Plowing by Day
House On The Wrong Side
Racing The Hat
3. The Uglest Duckling
4. Boys In Tatters
5. Homesteading
6. Tattered Boys And Tattered Years
7. Drama in the Sand (including "The Green Glass Floats" by Owen Betterton)
8. A Rose In The Thorn
9. Big Bash at Raft River
10. The Blue Ranch

2. Cotterel, Heglar, and Albion
Hymn of Harrison Valley
Buster Hound
One Nightengale, One Frog
11. Hard Times
12. The Cotterel Bride
13. The Spellcasters (Rain Follows the Plow)
14. Sons of the Land
15. Lost in a Storm
16. Snake Killer from Cheyenne
17. Taming the Wild
18. Baseballs and Hatchets
19. Rolling Up the Wire
20. The White Horse
21. Jenny and the Gypsy
22. Blind Barns
23. Flight From Cotterel
24. A Plat, A Town, A Dream

3. Jack Simplot's Empire
The Golden Dulcimer
See Here!
25. Declo and the Mountains Beyond
26. Father and the Financier
27. John Hill's Smithy
28. The Three-Hundred-Watt Blues
29. Rivers Settlers
30. Run Rabbit Run
31. The Magic Touch
32. Roy's Café
33. Ol' Brown
34. Walker Hall
35. When Buck Rode the Celluloid Trail
36. Valentino
37. Hollywood Halo—Silence and Sound
38. Prairie Comedians

4. The Marble Parrot & Other Tales
The Rebel
The Parting
39. The Face that Never Laughed
40. Kino
41. Gross Neglect
42. Louie and the Snake
43. Balboa Park
44. The Marble Parrot
45. The Kitchen Sink: The Pothole; Cotterel Wilderness; Class of '31; Rich, Choke, Lean; Bill, Man of Mystery; Gingerbread Brown; The Flaccus Boys
46. Elk Mountain Miracle
47. The Lost Hawaiians
48. Faris Hall
49. Sawyer's

Epilogue
Those Little Blue Books, and The Rise and Demise of E. Haldeman-Julius

Lightning Source grayscale test. A *full spectrum* of experience courtesy of Scandia Patch Press.